Mr Twiddle Stories

Mr Twiddle is _____
minded _____
memb_____
so he g_____
His bu_____ _____ y
cross, bu_____ gh.

Enid B_____ no introduction to
her reader. Author of around four
hundred books, which have been trans-
lated into almost every language, she
has been known and loved by children
of all ages for many years.

Other Enid Blyton titles available in Beaver

MR TWIDDLE STORIES

Enid Blyton

Illustrated by Rene Cloke

Beaver Books

A Beaver Book
Published by Arrow Books Limited
62–5 Chandos Place, London WC2N 4NW

An imprint of Century Hutchinson Ltd

London Melbourne Sydney Auckland
Johannesburg and agencies throughout
the world

First published in Beaver as two volumes,
Hello, Mr Twiddle! and *Well, Really, Mr Twiddle!*, in 1982
Reprinted 1984
This edition 1989

Printed and bound in Great Britain by
Cox & Wyman Ltd, Reading

ISBN 0 09 965560 8

1. HELLO MR TWIDDLE!

Contents

1

Mr Twiddle and the cow

One day Mrs Twiddle asked Mr Twiddle to go and fetch her brother's cow for her.

'Albert, my brother, is going away,' she said, 'and I told him we would look after his cow for a day or two, Twiddle. So you go and fetch it, and we'll keep it in the field behind the house. It will be nice to have some fresh milk for nothing.'

Mr Twiddle put down his paper and got up with a sigh. There always seemed something to do just when he was nicely settled. He brushed his hair, stuffed a clean handkerchief into his pocket, and went to the door.

'Twiddle, don't forget your hat,' said Mrs Twiddle. 'I believe you'd forget to take your head with you if it wasn't so firmly fixed on.'

'I don't want my hat,' said Mr Twiddle.

'You *must* take your hat!' said Mrs Twiddle firmly. 'The sun is going to be hot.'

So Twiddle had to take his hat. But he felt rather obstinate that morning and he made up his mind that although he had to take his hat, he wouldn't wear it. No, he'd carry it in his hand! Aha, Mrs Twiddle, you'd be cross if you saw that!

It was a nice hat, for it was a new one. It was brown, and had a fine brown ribbon round it, tied in a bow at the side. It fitted Mr Twiddle perfectly. Secretly Mr Twiddle thought he looked extremely nice in his new hat, and he quite meant to put it on if he met anyone. But he didn't.

He got to the field and called the cow. The cow, a gentle creature who knew him well, came to the gate at once. Mr Twiddle tied a rope round her neck and led her off.

He hadn't gone far before his shoelace came undone. Mr Twiddle looked down at it. He had his hat in one hand and the cow's rope in the other. What was he to do?

'I must just hang my hat up somewhere,' said Mr Twiddle, in a dreamy voice, for he was hot and rather sleepy. He looked for something to hang his hat up on, and saw the cow's horns, looking just like the hall pegs at home on which he always hung his hat.

Mr Twiddle put his hat on the horns of the surprised cow. Then he knelt down and did up his shoelace, very cleverly, with one hand.

'Ha!' he said proudly, when he had finished. 'Some folks may call me a stupid man – but it isn't many who could tie a lace with one hand!'

He walked on with the cow, feeling quite pleased with himself. The cow came gently after him, wearing the brown hat, looking very comical indeed. But Mr Twiddle had forgotten all about his hat.

It wasn't until the sun shone down really hotly on his head that he felt he needed a hat. He put his hand up to his head and found no hat there. He looked at his two hands. Now what had happened to his hat? He had certainly started out with it!

'Oh, bother, bother, bother!' said Mr Twiddle. 'I must have left it on the gate where I fetched the cow!'

So back he went, the cow still following, Mr Twiddle's hat perched up on her horns. Soon they met Mrs Gabble, and how she laughed to see the cow!

'Sorry I can't raise my hat to you this morning,' said Mr Twiddle politely, 'but I've put it somewhere and forgotten it!'

'Ho, ho, so you have!' giggled Mrs Gabble, and she laughed till the tears ran down her cheek.

The next person Mr Twiddle met was Dame Shoo, and she looked quite alarmed when she saw Mr Twiddle without a hat and the cow with one.

'Just going to look for my hat, Dame Shoo,' said Mr Twiddle politely. 'You know, I've left it somewhere about, and I must find it.'

'Ask the cow and maybe she'll tell you where it is,' said Dame Shoo with a squeal of laughter.

Mr Twiddle looked crossly at her. 'Silly woman!' he thought. 'Ask the cow indeed! As if *she* could tell me where my hat is!'

Then he met Mr Wonks, the hot-sausage man who sold ice creams in the summer.

'Good day, Mr Twiddle!' said Mr Wonks, grinning at the cow. 'Hot weather for the cow, isn't it! I see you don't want her to get a headache.'

Mr Twiddle stared at him in amazement. What *could* Mr Wonks mean?

'You must be mad, Mr Wonks,' said Mr Twiddle, in a high and mighty voice. 'Cows don't get headaches.'

'No, nor sunstroke either, by the look of things!' grinned Mr Wonks.

Mr Twiddle said no more. He began to think that the sun had made everyone a little mad this morning. He got to the field gate, but alas! there was no hat to be seen. Mr Twiddle was upset. Someone must have been along and taken it!

'My nice new hat too!' he said mournfully. 'What, oh what, will Mrs Twiddle say?'

He went home so upset that he didn't notice how

everyone laughed at the cow with the hat on. He took the cow round to the back door, to show Mrs Twiddle, for she was fond of the gentle creature.

As soon as Mrs Twiddle opened the door, Mr Twiddle began to explain about his hat.

'I'm so very sorry,' he said, 'but somehow or other I seem to have lost my hat. Maybe it blew away – maybe someone stole it – I don't know what happened. But, anyway, I'm very sorry, my dear, and I'll go and buy a new one this very minute. I do wish I knew what had happened to it.'

'If you look behind you, you'll see that the cow had more sense than you,' cried his wife. 'She knew how to bring a hat home, anyhow!'

Twiddle turned and looked at the cow. He saw his hat perched on her horns. The cow opened her mouth and spoke gently.

'Moo-oo!' she said, 'moo-oo!' And she waggled her

head gently, asking Mr Twiddle to take off the hat, for it annoyed her.

'Oh, the clever creature!' cried Mr Twiddle, in the greatest delight. 'Mrs Twiddle, do you see, she has got my hat for me! She must have found it and put it on, and brought it all the way home for me! Now isn't that really remarkably clever? I must go and tell everyone about this most extraordinary cow.'

And with that Mr Twiddle beamed all over his face, gave his wife a good slap and kissed the cow on the nose.

'Sorry, dear, sorry!' he said, as he saw Mrs Twiddle looking as black as thunder. 'I meant to kiss you and slap the cow, I did really!'

And, clapping his hat on his head upside down, he hurried off to tell everyone the story of how the cow had found his hat and worn it home. Dear old Twiddle, he *is* a muddler, isn't he!

2

Mr Twiddle gets a shock

Mr Twiddle was always doing something silly. Well, did you ever hear the tale of what happened when he threw his handkerchief into the fire by mistake?

I'll tell you. It happened one morning when Mr Twiddle was opening his letters by the kitchen fire. 'You can throw the envelopes into the fire,' said Mrs Twiddle. 'It will save me fetching the wastepaper basket.'

Well, Mr Twiddle at that moment felt he was going to sneeze, so, with an envelope in one hand and his best white silk handkerchief in the other, he sat in his chair, waiting for the sneeze to come.

And when it *did* come – a-TISH-oo-ish-oo! – Mr Twiddle caught the sneeze in the envelope, and threw his handkerchief, quite by mistake, into the fire!

Well, of course, he was terribly upset as soon as he had done this, and tried to rake his handkerchief out of the fire! A bit of burning coal fell on the rug and scorched a hole at once. Mrs Twiddle came running in when she smelt the smell of burning – and how she scolded Mr Twiddle!

'Catching a sneeze in an envelope and throwing your best handkerchief on the fire!' she snorted, pouring water on the burning rug. 'Whatever will you do next, Twiddle? Don't you know the difference between a handkerchief and an envelope? You'll be poking the fire with your pencil and trying to write with the poker next! You might have had the whole house on fire. Go out for a walk, do, and don't come in till dinner time!'

Poor Mr Twiddle! He was really very unhappy about his best handkerchief. He got up, found his hat, put it on back to front and went into the village. And very soon he met old Mrs Gabble, who always loved a chat. When she saw Mr Twiddle looking so upset, she stopped.

'What's the matter?' she said.

'Oh,' said Mr Twiddle, 'a dreadful thing happened this morning. I threw my handkerchief on the fire by mistake, and it got burnt, and when I tried to get it out of the flames, some burning coal fell on the carpet and. . . .'

'Good gracious me!' said Mrs Gabble, 'no wonder you feel upset!' Then she caught sight of Sally Simple and she hurried to tell her the news. But, of course, she added a bit to it to make it even more exciting!

'Oh, Sally Simple,' she cried, 'have you heard what happened at the Twiddles' house this morning? Why, poor old Twiddle threw his handkerchief on the fire by mistake and, in getting it out, the fire fell on to the rug and set it all ablaze!'

'Goodness me!' said Sally, quite frightened. 'And did the kitchen catch alight?'

'I expect so,' said Mrs Gabble happily. 'Oh yes, I am sure it blazed up on to the ceiling!'

Sally Simple was thrilled. She longed to tell someone about the fire at the Twiddles'. She saw Dame Shoo over the way and rushed to tell her.

'Oh, Dame Shoo,' she cried, 'have you heard of the terrible fire at poor Mrs Twiddle's this morning?'

'No,' said Dame Shoo, startled. 'What about it?'

'Oh, Mr Twiddle dropped his handkerchief in the

fire, and that started a dreadful burning,' said Sally
Simple. 'Yes, the rug caught fire, and the flames shot
up to the ceiling! The whole kitchen was on fire.'

'But how dreadful!' said Dame Shoo. 'I suppose
the house will be burnt down?'

'Yes, sure to be,' said Sally Simple. 'I do wonder if
the fire engines have gone to see to it. And don't you
think we ought to offer to give the Twiddles' a bed
for tonight, because, with their house burnt down,
they'll have nowhere to sleep!'

'Yes, yes!' said Dame Shoo. 'I'll go and tell everyone else, Sally, and we'll see what we can do.'

She hurried off, longing to tell someone the news.

On the way she passed the fire station. She peeped
inside – and to her very great surprise she saw the big
fire engine still there. It hadn't gone to the Twiddles'!

'I say! I say!' cried Dame Shoo, rushing into the
fire station in a great hurry. 'Haven't you heard of the

dreadful fire at the Twiddles' house? It will be burnt to nothing if you don't hurry at once!'

'First we've heard of it!' cried the captain of the fire brigade, and he sounded the big fire bell at once.

In three minutes every fireman was in his place, complete with helmet. With a loud clanging of bells the great red fire engine roared out of the building.

Clang! Clang! Clang! It sped away to Mr Twiddle's house. Everyone ran after it to see where it was going. It stopped outside Mr Twiddle's house. The firemen undid the long hose and looked for the fire.

Mrs Twiddle looked out of the window. She saw the fire engine. She saw the firemen unwinding the hose. She saw the crowds and crowds of people. Whatever had they all come for?

She opened the door and looked out.

'Hie, Mrs Twiddle, where's the fire?' shouted the men.

'What fire?' asked Mrs Twiddle, in the greatest astonishment.

'The fire we've come to put out!' said the men.

'Well, there's only one fire in the house and that's in the kitchen grate,' said Mrs Twiddle, even more astonished. 'And I'm sure I don't want *that* put out, thank you!'

At that moment Mr Twiddle walked up, looking as surprised as could be to see such a crowd round his house.

'You said there was a terrible fire in your house!' cried Dame Shoo.

'I didn't!' said Mr Twiddle indignantly.

'You did!' shouted everyone.

'I only told Mrs Gabble I had burnt my handkerchief by mistake!' shouted Mr Twiddle, and he went inside and banged the door.

The fire engine turned round and drove off in disgust. Everyone went home. Mrs Twiddle stared at Mr Twiddle crossly.

'Do you need to bring the fire engine here and half the town, just because you happen to have burnt your handkerchief?' she said. 'Really, Mr Twiddle! Please don't do any more foolish things today.'

'Don't worry. I *shan't*!' said Mr Twiddle gloomily, and he threw his hat into the wastepaper basket and hung up his newspaper on a peg.

Well, really, Mr Twiddle!

Mr Twiddle fetches the fish

'Mr Twiddle, Mr Twiddle, the fish boy hasn't been with the fish!' called Mrs Twiddle. 'Just put on your coat and go and fetch it for me, will you! And you might get the newspaper at the same time, because it hasn't been left this morning.'

Mr Twiddle jumped up at once. He had missed his newspaper very much, and he was pleased to go and fetch it. Yes, he would fetch the fish as well – it was on the way to the newspaper shop.

He went off, humming, looking forward to a nice lazy morning with his newspaper when he got back. Ah, there was nothing like a good fat newspaper and a nice brown pipe! Mrs Twiddle would be pleased with him for fetching the fish, and would let him read in peace.

He came to the fish shop and called the man. 'Can I have Mrs Twiddle's fish, please?' he asked. 'It hasn't come.'

'Certainly, sir, certainly,' said the man. 'Five herrings, isn't it? Here they are!'

He took a newspaper, slapped the five slippery herrings into it, and rolled them up. He gave the parcel to Mr Twiddle, who slipped it under his arm. He set off to the newspaper shop.

'My newspaper, please,' he said to the man. 'You forgot to leave it this morning.'

'Sorry, sir!' said the man, and he rolled up

Mr Twiddle's newspaper and gave it to him. Mr Twiddle put it under his other arm.

Then he set off home, whistling softly. Ah, it would be nice to sit down in his armchair by the fire, unfold his newspaper, light his pipe, and puff away in peace, whilst Mrs Twiddle cooked herrings, and he smelt the delicious smell of them!

He reached home, and slapped down his newspaper on the table. 'Fish, Mrs Twiddle, fish!' he said. 'Good fat herrings for dinner!'

He didn't notice that he had put his own newspaper on the table, and had put the parcel of fish on his chair. The fish was wrapped in a newspaper too, so it wasn't a difficult mistake to make.

Mr Twiddle went to get his pipe. Mrs Twiddle unrolled the newspaper he had put on the table. She looked astonished, and then called to Mr Twiddle:

'Twiddle! What have you done with the fish? It isn't here!'

'Isn't there!' said Twiddle in alarm. 'But it must be! I saw the man slap the herrings into the paper myself!'

'Then they must have dropped out, Mr Twiddle,' said Mrs Twiddle crossly. 'Just like you! You'd better go back and get some more.'

Mr Twiddle stared in dismay. 'But I want to read and to smoke my pipe!' he said. 'I'm tired!'

'Well, sit down for five minutes and rest,' said Mrs Twiddle. 'Then you must go, or we will have nothing for dinner.'

Twiddle sighed. Something always seemed to go wrong. He looked for his newspaper. Ah yes, he had put it in his armchair. The cat was there too, scraping hard at the paper. It could smell the fish in it, of course! But Mr Twiddle didn't know that. He thought it was just his newspaper and nothing else.

'Look at the cat!' he said to his wife. 'I believe she's trying to open the newspaper and read it!'

'Fiddlesticks!' said Mrs Twiddle snappily. 'Whatever will you say next? You'll tell me the canary wants to smoke your pipe!'

Mr Twiddle lighted his pipe. Then he took up the newspaper from the chair and sat down. He shook out the paper – and out fell five slippery herrings, all down Mr Twiddle's nice clean waistcoat and trousers!

'Bless us all, what's this!' shouted Mr Twiddle in a fright, jumping up. 'Mrs Twiddle, Mrs Twiddle, there's something hiding in my newspaper – big earwigs, or something! Ooo-ooo-oooh! They all jumped out at me when I opened my paper!'

The cat jumped at the fish in delight. She sat down and began to eat it. Mr Twiddle beamed at her.

'Look at that now!' he cried. 'The cat's attacking them! Clever creature!'

Mrs Twiddle hurried in and gave a shout of dismay. 'It's the herrings!' she cried. 'Twiddle, are you mad? What have you given them to the cat for? Shoo, puss, shoo!'

The cat shooed. Mr Twiddle looked foolish. Mrs Twiddle picked up the herrings, scolding all the while.

'Really, what shall I do with you, Twiddle! Giving me your newspaper, and trying to read the herrings, and then giving them to the cat! Well, there will be one less for your dinner now, for the cat's had one.'

'I did *not* give them to the cat,' said Mr Twiddle crossly.

'You did!' said Mrs Twiddle. 'Didn't I see you beaming at the cat eating the herrings when I came in?'

'Well,' said Mr Twiddle, cheering up suddenly, 'I needn't go off to the fish shop again, because the fish are found. So I can read my newspaper in peace! Where is it?'

'Oh, I've torn it up to make new paper to line the larder shelves,' said Mrs Twiddle. 'If you want to read it you'll have to go and stand in the larder and read the news on each shelf, Mr Twiddle. That will teach you to give herrings to the cat again!'

Poor Twiddle! He spent all the morning in the larder, reading the news on each shelf, for Mrs Twiddle had torn up the paper and spread it neatly there. He couldn't even have his pipe, for he wasn't allowed to smoke one in the larder. He really is the funniest old thing, isn't he!

4

Mr Twiddle and the snowman

One day the children who lived next door to Mr Twiddle made a fine snowman in his garden. Mrs Twiddle said they might, because her garden was so much bigger than theirs. So the children were very pleased, and they built a big man, quite as tall as their Daddy, and very fat and round.

'Mrs Twiddle, Mrs Twiddle, can we have an old hat for his head, and an old scarf for his neck?' called the children, looking in at the kitchen window, where Mrs Twiddle was making cakes.

'Yes,' said Mrs Twiddle. 'You'll find an old hat in the hall, and a ragged old scarf somewhere by it. And if you look in the hall drawer you'll maybe find an old pair of gloves too, for the snowman's cold hands!'

'Oh, good!' shouted the children, and they tore off to get the clothes. They found them all – and they found Mr Twiddle's stick too, which they borrowed for their funny old snowman.

My word, he did look grand when he was finished and dressed up! You should have seen him, with Mr Twiddle's old hat on his head, a scarf tied loosely round his fat neck, raggedy gloves on his round hands, and a stick through his arm! Really, he looked very fine indeed, and the children were proud of him.

Mrs Twiddle looked out of the window and laughed. 'He just wants a pipe to stick in his mouth,'

she said, 'then he'll be happy. Here is one of Mr Twiddle's.'

So the children stuck a pipe in the snowman's mouth, and then danced round him, laughing. Their mother rang the tea bell next door, and they hurried off, hungry and happy, wondering what Mr Twiddle would say when he saw their wonderful snowman.

Well, Mr Twiddle didn't come home till it was almost dark, for he had been to see his brother in the next village. He stumped in at the front gate, tired and hungry – and then he suddenly saw the old snowman standing quite still in his front garden.

'Hallo!' said Mr Twiddle, in surprise. 'Who's that? What are you doing here, my good man?'

The good man didn't answer. Mr Twiddle grew cross.

'You needn't think I can't see you, standing there, trying to hide from me in the darkness!' he said. 'You are up to no good, I'll be bound! What are you waiting there for?'

The snowman said nothing at all. Mr Twiddle marched right up to him and looked at him as closely as he could in the half-darkness. And he saw that the snowman had got *his* hat on!

'You've got my hat!' he said, in a rage. 'My dear old comfortable hat! How dare you take my hat! Give it to me at once!'

The snowman didn't give it to Mr Twiddle. He just stood quite still and stared at him out of his big stone eyes.

'And you've got my scarf on, I do declare!' roared Mr Twiddle. 'Yes, you have! What next, I'd like to know! I suppose you've been sneaking round my house, just taking whatever you can put your hands on! I'll fetch a policeman! I'll give you such a smack that you'll land in the next-door garden!'

The snowman stared and said nothing. 'Can't you answer me?' shouted Mr Twiddle. 'Haven't you got a tongue in your head?'

The poor old snowman hadn't got a tongue of any sort, so he couldn't say a word. He just stood there in Mr Twiddle's hat and scarf, looking very large and miserable.

'And if you haven't got my gloves and my stick!' cried Mr Twiddle, suddenly seeing them in darkness, and feeling them. 'This is too much! My hat, my scarf – and now my gloves and my stick! You are a wicked robber, and if you don't give me back my things at once, this very minute, I'll go out and get a policeman! Now!'

The snowman didn't move. Then a bit of snow melted by his mouth and his pipe fell out. Mr Twiddle picked it up.

'And you've got my pipe too!' he shouted. 'My very

nicest, oldest pipe! What next! Are you wearing my vests and my socks and my best shirt under that large white overcoat of yours? Oh, you bad, wicked robber!'

Just then the village policeman came by and heard the shouting. He walked into the front garden.

'Now then, what's all this?' he asked.

'Oh, policeman, I'm glad you've come,' said Mr Twiddle. 'This robber won't give me back my clothes that he's stolen. He must be deaf and dumb, for he won't even say a word to me.'

Mr Twiddle suddenly slipped on the snow and fell against the snowman. He clutched at him and one of the snowman's stone buttons fell off and hit Mr Twiddle sharply on the nose.

'Oh, you wicked fellow, you hit me!' shouted Mr Twiddle, in a rage. 'Take that—and that—and that!'

He slapped the snowman hard, and the snow fell off in big pieces. Mr Twiddle was astonished. He hit the snowman again, and the funny old snowman began to fall to bits. Mr Twiddle fell on top of him and floundered about in the snow, shouting and smacking. The policeman pulled him up, just as Mrs Twiddle came to the door in astonishment, holding a lantern to see what was the matter.

'Twiddle! What are you doing?' she called. 'Are you being rude to the policeman?'

'No, Mam, he isn't,' said the policeman, with a grin. 'He's fighting a big snowman and breaking him all to bits!'

'Really, Mr Twiddle!' said Mrs Twiddle, in surprise. '*Must* you do a thing like that? And look at the mess you're in! Good gracious me—and you've spoilt your new hat and broken your nice new stick! Well, you'll have to use your old ones again. The snowman has got them, so you can bring them in with you before he melts all over them.'

Poor Mr Twiddle! He couldn't think of a word to say – not a word! He went into the kitchen, all covered with snow, and Mrs Twiddle shooed him out again.

'I'm not going to let you cover my nice kitchen floor with melting snow!' she cried. 'Shake yourself in the yard, please! And chop up your broken stick – it will do for firewood!'

Mr Twiddle went to the woodshed very gloomily. He took the chopper – and, oh dear me, he chopped up his hat, and then went to hang his broken stick on the peg! There really is no knowing what he'll do next!

5

Mr Twiddle makes a muddle

Once upon a time Mrs Twiddle got very tired of having Mr Twiddle in the house.

'Mr Twiddle, for goodness sake go out into the garden and do some work!' she cried. 'Do you know what you've been doing all the morning? You've been trying to smoke your fountain pen, and you've put your pipe into the inkstand! And is it you who has stood the poker in the hall stand and put your umbrella in the fender?'

'Oh dear! Oh dear!' said Mr Twiddle, taking his fountain pen out of his mouth and staring at it. 'I thought my pipe tasted a bit funny today. I'll go out and do a bit of gardening, Mrs Twiddle.'

'You'd better, before you start to poke the fire with your umbrella,' said Mrs Twiddle. 'Your best one, too! Really, Twiddle, why don't you use your brains?'

Mr Twiddle could hear by the way that his wife talked that she was not in a very good temper. So he quickly went into the hall, put on his goloshes, tied his old scarf round his neck, and ran out of doors.

It was cold. What should he do? He poked his head into the shed. It was dark there, but he could see something piled up in a corner.

'Bless us all!' said Mr Twiddle, staring. 'I believe those are daffodil bulbs we've forgotten to plant. Dear, dear! — what would Mrs Twiddle say if she knew all those were sprouting away there in the

corner, instead of growing into nice yellow daffodils for the spring? Now, it would be a good thing if I planted them all. That would keep me busy all the morning.'

So he took his spade and set to work. He dug up the bed, and then fetched the bulbs in his barrow. He set them all in nice rows, and covered them up gently with earth. Oh, he could work well when he liked, could Mr Twiddle. He quite enjoyed himself, for the morning was fine.

He planted every single bulb, and then he heard his wife calling him.

'You seem to be working very hard, Mr Twiddle. I suppose you will be hungry for dinner. Would you like a nice stew with carrots and onions and turnips?'

'Oooh, yes!' said Mr Twiddle, feeling quite hungry at the thought.

'Well, fetch me a few carrots, one large turnip, and some onions from the shed,' called Mrs Twiddle. So Mr Twiddle went to the shed and looked round. The carrots were in a basket, and so were a few turnips. He put them into a box and looked round for the onions. He couldn't see a single one. He trotted back to the house.

'There are no onions at all,' he said.

'Rubbish!' said Mrs Twiddle. 'There are heaps. Go back and look again, Twiddle.'

So Mr Twiddle went back and looked again. But still he couldn't see any onions, although this time he looked up at the roof of the shed too, thinking they might be hung there. He trotted back to the house again.

'I'm sorry, Mrs Twiddle, but really and truly there are no onions there!' he said.

'Mr Twiddle, you make me cross!' said Mrs Twiddle. 'Why, I put the onions in the shed myself!

I'll come and show you. Really, I should have thought you knew an onion by now.'

Mrs Twiddle went down to the shed with Mr Twiddle.

She looked all round – and then she stared in surprise.

'How strange!' she said. 'How very, very strange! Not a single onion here! Where have they all gone? You haven't been eating them, Twiddle, have you?'

'Of course not,' said Mr Twiddle, offended. 'I don't eat raw onions. Whereabouts did you put them?'

'In that corner,' said Mrs Twiddle, pointing. 'They were there yesterday – a whole heap of them. Wherever can they have gone to?'

Mr Twiddle stared at the corner where his wife was pointing – and a horrid cold feeling came over him. There *had* been something in that corner this morning – and he had planted it – dozens and dozens and dozens!

'What are you looking like that for, Mr Twiddle?' asked Mrs Twiddle, staring at him. 'Have you done something to my onions?'

'Nothing very much, dear,' said Mr Twiddle, trying to smile. 'I – well – I just planted them all, that's all!'

'*Planted* them, Twiddle!' said Mrs Twiddle, in the greatest surprise. 'What did you want to plant onions for? You helped me yourself to pull them up from the ground in the autumn! Why did you plant them again?'

'I thought they were bulbs,' said Mr Twiddle.

'Well, they *are* bulbs!' said Mrs Twiddle, 'but they are not the sort to plant in the garden.'

'I thought they were daffodils,' said poor Mr Twiddle. 'I've been very, very hard at work all the morning, planting them in neat rows. I thought it would be such a surprise for you.'

'Well, it certainly *is* a surprise,' said Mrs Twiddle. 'And now, Twiddle, I'm afraid if you want any onions in your stew for dinner, you'll have to do some more hard work and dig up those onions again!'

Poor Mr Twiddle. He sadly took up his spade and dug up all the dozens and dozens and dozens of onions he had so carefully planted that morning! And wasn't he hungry when he had finished! 'I could eat two whole stews, I declare!' he said to Mrs Twiddle, when he went in.

There was a beautiful stew for him, and he did enjoy it.

'I'm sorry you had your work all for nothing, Twiddle,' said Mrs Twiddle, as she gave him a fourth helping of the stew. 'But, my dear man, do try and think what you're doing in future.'

'Oh, I will, Mrs Twiddle, I will!' said Mr Twiddle, picking up the sugar-sifter and shaking sugar all over his stew instead of the pepper. 'I've quite made up my mind about that!'

And he stirred his lemonade with the salt spoon, smiling all over his funny old face! You just can't stop him from doing things like that, can you!

6

Mr Twiddle in the rain

Once Mr Twiddle wanted to go and call on a friend of his and borrow a book. So he knocked out his pipe, put down his newspaper, and got up.

'Where are you going, Twiddle?' asked Mrs Twiddle.

'I'm going to Mr Twisty's,' said Mr Twiddle. 'He's got a most exciting book I want to borrow – all about pirates.'

'But it's pouring with rain, Twiddle!' said Mrs Twiddle. 'You'll get soaked!'

'Oh no, I'll put on my mackintosh and take my umbrella,' said Twiddle. 'I shall be all right.'

He went into the hall, thinking about the book of pirates. He took down his mackintosh and put it on. He wasn't thinking at all of what he was doing, and when he saw his coat hanging on its usual peg, he put that on, too, over his mackintosh. Then he hunted for his umbrella.

There it was in the umbrella stand. Good! Mr Twiddle took it out. He went to the front door and put up his umbrella. He walked down the path – but he had got no farther than the front gate when he heard Mrs Twiddle knocking on the window.

'What do you want?' shouted Twiddle.

'You want your *mackintosh* on!' shouted Mrs Twiddle. 'You said you would put it on! Come and do so!'

Mr Twiddle stared down at himself in astonishment. 'But I did put it on!' he called back.

'Twiddle, don't be silly,' said Mrs Twiddle, and she hurried to the front door and opened it. 'Come back at once. You can see quite well you've got your overcoat on. What's the use of a mac if you don't use it when it's raining?'

Twiddle walked back, shut his umbrella, and looked for his mackintosh. Of course, as he already had it on under his coat, it was nowhere to be found.

'Well!' said Twiddle in amazement, 'it was certainly hanging on its peg in the hall when I came out of the kitchen just now. Where's it gone?'

'Mackintoshes can't walk,' said Mrs Twiddle, busy looking everywhere. 'Now where in the world have you put that mackintosh, Mr Twiddle?'

Well, Mr and Mrs Twiddle hunted everywhere. Twiddle went upstairs into his bedroom and took everything out of his wardrobe. Then he went downstairs and out into the gardener's shed to see if by any chance he had left it there.

And whilst he was there he hung his umbrella up on a peg with all the spades and forks. But he couldn't find his mackintosh. So indoors he went again, leaving his umbrella out in the shed.

When he got indoors he wanted to use his handkerchief to catch a sneeze in. So he undid his coat and tried to find his trousers pocket – but, of course, his mackintosh was underneath and he couldn't seem to get his pocket at all.

Mrs Twiddle looked to see what he was struggling about – and saw his mackintosh under his coat!

'Twiddle!' she cried. 'If you aren't the most tiresome man under the sun! *There's* your mackintosh!'

'Where?' asked Twiddle, looking all round him

and up on the ceiling too, as if he expected to see it flying around.

'On your own self!' cried Mrs Twiddle. 'You put it on – and then put your coat over it! Good gracious, I do believe you'll forget your own head one day and go walking off without it!'

'Well, my dear, you needn't say any more,' said Twiddle. 'It was just a mistake. After all, this hall is so dark that it's not to be wondered at if I put my mac on first and then my coat. Well, I'll go. It's still raining very hard, so I'll take off my coat and just have my mac on.'

'And what about your umbrella?' asked Mrs

39

Twiddle, looking in the umbrella stand. 'Where's that gone now? You had it over your arm a few minutes ago.'

'Oh, it's about somewhere,' said Twiddle, looking round anxiously. Really, it was most extraordinary the way his things seemed to vanish! That umbrella was really nowhere to be seen!

'Well, I can't waste all my morning getting you ready to go out into the rain,' said Mrs Twiddle. 'I've got to peel some potatoes for dinner.'

She left Twiddle standing in the hall, looking everywhere for his lost umbrella. She took a basket and went out to the shed for some potatoes.

Mrs Twiddle filled her basket, and was just going out of the shed when she happened to look up – and she caught sight of Twiddle's umbrella hanging on a peg beside a spade and a fork. She stared at it in the greatest surprise. Then she went quickly into the house.

'Twiddle! Twiddle!' she called. 'You must have thought your umbrella was a rake or a hoe! You've hung it up with the tools in the shed!'

Well, really! Poor Mr Twiddle! He stared at Mrs Twiddle as if he couldn't believe his ears. Then, very red indeed, he went to the shed to get his umbrella. He came back with it.

He had made up his mind to be really sensible now. He would even put on his goloshes!

So he hunted for them and put them on. He did up his mac. He put up his umbrella and set off down the path just as the clock was striking one.

Mrs Twiddle called to him. 'Twiddle! Can't you see that the sun is shining hotly now and that the rain is over? You *do* look foolish in your mac and goloshes and umbrella! Also, don't you want any lunch? It's one o'clock, and I've just put it on the table!'

'Dear, dear! I've got to go without that pirate book!' groaned Twiddle. And he hung his goloshes on his coat peg, stuck his mac into the umbrella stand, and put his umbrella into the boot cupboard. Do you suppose he *ever* thinks what he is doing?

7

Mr Twiddle's bonfires

Guy Fawkes Day was coming near. Mr Twiddle stopped and looked each morning in the toy shop, which had a wonderful show of brightly coloured fireworks in the window.

Now Mr Twiddle loved fireworks – but Mrs Twiddle didn't. She said they were noisy, bangy things that left a lot of rubbish behind them in the garden. So for many years Mr Twiddle had had to listen to other people's fireworks, and hadn't had any of his own.

But this year he had a good idea. He would buy some for the children next door! Ah, that really *was* a fine idea! Then Mr Twiddle could look out of the window and see the children letting off the fireworks – and it would be as good as setting them off himself!

So on Bonfire Day he went to the toy shop and bought a fine collection. There were six rockets, four Roman candles, any amount of squibs, four large catherine wheels, and a great many little odd fireworks that he didn't know the name of. The man put them into a big paper bag and gave them to Mr Twiddle.

When he got home he found that Mrs Twiddle had put on her gardening boots and coat, and was going down the garden.

'Oh, there you are, Twiddle,' she said. 'Put on your gardening boots too, and come along with me.

It's quite time we took down the old beanpoles and sweet-pea sticks and burnt them all, along with the other rubbish. It's a fine afternoon, so it will do us good.'

'Right,' said Twiddle, and he put on his old boots. He went down the garden, carrying his bag of fireworks, for he meant to hand them over the fence to the children when he saw them. He popped them into his wheelbarrow, and went to fetch his fork.

Mr and Mrs Twiddle worked hard. They took up all the old poles and sticks, put aside those that would do for another year, and threw the others on to the bonfire. What a lot of rubbish there was! Old stems of cut-down plants, rotten potatoes, bad apples — oh, a heap of things that badly needed burning.

'If there's one thing I do like,' said Mr Twiddle, building up the rubbish heap, 'it's a good bonfire!'

He pushed a sheet of newspaper at the bottom of the heap and set a light to it. It flared up and the bonfire began to burn merrily, for Mr Twiddle really was good at getting bonfires going. He leaned on his fork and watched the fire.

Soon it began to die down. Mr Twiddle called to his wife:

'Bring some more rubbish. It wants feeding a little.'

Mrs Twiddle piled some old sticks into the wheelbarrow and wheeled it to the fire. She tipped the barrow over and everything went on to the burning heap. Mr Twiddle forked it into the heart of the bonfire.

'That's fine,' he said, pleased. 'My word, wife, hark at the crackling!'

But there was soon something else to listen to besides the crackling! For Mrs Twiddle had emptied the bag of fireworks on to the bonfire too! Right into the heart of the fire they went, and Twiddle forked them well in, not knowing that they were his precious fireworks.

The flames caught hold of them. They burnt a rocket. BANG! Whoooooosh! The rocket flew out of the bonfire like an aeroplane and took Mrs Twiddle's hat off. She gasped and screamed.

'Twiddle! What was that? Oh, what was that?'

A shower of stars showed up at the end of the garden. It was the end of the rocket. Then BANG! Another one went off, and shot out of the fire between Twiddle's legs, knocking away his fork as it went.

'Oooooh!' said Twiddle in the greatest surprise.

He jumped well away quickly as another rocket soared over his back, showering him with coloured stars!

The catherine wheels spluttered and fizzed. The Roman candles exploded with a roar. The squibs and other little fireworks went off bang and jumped out of the flames as if they were alive!

'Save us! What's all this?' screamed poor Mrs Twiddle, jumping out of the way of a firework that seemed to want to hop on her toes all the time. 'Ow! Get away, you horrid thing! Oh, there it is again! *Will* you get away?'

Twiddle stared in surprise at the bonfire. Then he suddenly guessed what had happened. Mrs Twiddle had emptied his fireworks on the fire!

'Oh, you threw all the fireworks I bought for the children next door on to the bonfire!' he cried. 'You silly woman!'

'Silly woman, indeed!' said Mrs Twiddle angrily.

'Why didn't you tell me you had got fireworks in your barrow? Silly man! Very, very silly man!'

'Well, I must buy some more for the children,' said Twiddle, jumping out of the way of a rocket. 'I'm tired of this. I'm going in.'

'Twiddle, just listen to *me*,' said Mrs Twiddle firmly. 'You are *not* going to waste your money on any more fireworks. As likely as not you'll throw them into the kitchen fire and then there'd be a fine to-do! Not another penny are you to spend on fireworks. Do you hear?'

'Very well,' said Twiddle meekly. He was very sad as he went indoors. Now he wouldn't be able to see any fireworks after all.

But cheer up, Mr Twiddle! The children have bought plenty for themselves, and if only you go upstairs to your bedroom window, you'll see them all! So cheer up, Mr Twiddle.

8

Mr Twiddle's mistake

At ten o'clock every night Mr Twiddle let in the cat, and took the dog out to his kennel. If he ever forgot, Mrs Twiddle always reminded him. The cat was usually waiting outside to come in, and the dog was usually quite ready to go out to his nice cosy kennel, lined with warm straw.

One night, at ten o'clock, Mrs Twiddle looked at Mr Twiddle. He was fast asleep in his chair, his head nodding over his book.

'Twiddle!' said Mrs Twiddle sharply. 'Wake up! It's ten o'clock. Time for BED.'

'Ooooomph!' said Mr Twiddle, opening his eyes with a jerk. 'Er – what did you say, my dear? I wasn't asleep.'

'Oh yes you were, Twiddle,' said his wife, folding up her knitting. 'Come along now. It's ten.'

So up they went to bed, Mr Twiddle still feeling very sleepy. He quite forgot about the dog and the cat. But Mrs Twiddle remembered.

'Twiddle! Have you let the cat in? And what about the dog?'

'Bother!' said Twiddle sleepily, putting his coat on once more. 'Well, I'll go down again.'

Down he went into the dark hall. He whistled to the dog to come to him. Then he opened the door. It was quite dark outside. Twiddle felt an animal against his legs and he thought it was the dog. But it

wasn't. The dog was lying on the couch, feeling
rather guilty because he hadn't answered Mr
Twiddle's whistle and gone to him. But he felt as if he
would rather sleep indoors that night, because it was
cold.

It was the cat that Mr Twiddle had felt! It had
come indoors and rubbed against his legs.

'Come on, come on!' said Twiddle, thinking it was
the dog. He went out into the yard, where the kennel
was. He couldn't see a thing, and he only knew he
had come to the kennel when he bumped into it.

The cat came with him, rubbing against him.

'Go into your kennel, Tinker,' said Twiddle, thinking he was talking to the dog. Usually he heard
Tinker's paws running into the kennel, but he didn't
hear them tonight.

So he put out his hand, touched something warm,
thought it was Tinker, and pushed him into the

49

kennel. But it was the cat he had pushed. Mr Twiddle shut the kennel door, as he always did on cold nights. Now the dog was safe!

He went back into the house and bolted the door. He went upstairs. The dog lay on the couch, feeling very guilty and ashamed of himself, and wondering why Mr Twiddle hadn't fetched him. And when Mr and Mrs Twiddle were fast asleep in bed, the dog crept upstairs to them.

He lay down under the bed, not daring to wake Mr Twiddle. He soon fell asleep.

But Tinker always snored when he lay on his tummy with his head on his paws. And soon he began to make his little dog snores. 'Ur-r-r-r-r-r! Ur-r-r-r-r-r!'

Mrs Twiddle woke up with a jump and sat up in bed. She listened.

'Ur-r-r-r-r!' went Tinker, dreaming of bones and biscuits.

'Twiddle!' said Mrs Twiddle in a fright. 'There's somebody in the room!'

Twiddle woke up in astonishment. He sat up too. The noise awoke Tinker under the bed and he sat up as well, and stopped snoring. There was silence, whilst all three of them listened.

'There's nobody, wife,' said Twiddle crossly. 'What did the noise sound like?'

'Well, it really sounded rather like Tinker snoring,' said Mrs Twiddle, puzzled. 'I suppose you *did* put the dog into his kennel, Twiddle?'

'Of course I did, *and* shut the door on him,' said Twiddle, settling down comfortably. 'Do go to sleep, wife.'

Mrs Twiddle lay down. Tinker lay down – but he made a big bump on the floor as he did so, and in a trice Mrs Twiddle sat up again.

'There! Did you hear that? It was a bump!' she cried. But Twiddle was asleep, so, as she heard nothing more, Mrs Twiddle lay down. But soon Tinker began to snore again, and Mrs Twiddle woke Twiddle by shaking him hard.

'There's that noise again!' she said. 'Oh, do wake up, Twiddle! This is dreadful!'

Twiddle awoke. He felt angry. He lay and listened, but as Tinker was now awake again, he didn't snore. He was still feeling ashamed of himself because he hadn't gone to his kennel. He wanted to lick his master and mistress and say he was sorry.

Very quietly, he crept from under the bed, and sniffed till he found Twiddle's hand hanging down by the bed.

He licked it with his warm wet tongue. Twiddle was most surprised. He simply could *not* imagine what the

wetness was. He didn't like it. He took his hand away.

Tinker was sad. He went to where Mrs Twiddle lay, on the other side of the bed. He put out his tongue and licked her nose.

'Ooooh!' squealed Mrs Twiddle in a fright, and sat up at once. 'Twiddle! Something licked me! I tell you something licked me! On my nose, too!'

'Funny,' said Twiddle. 'Something licked me too.'

'If Tinker wasn't in his kennel, I'd think it was he who was here,' said Mrs Twiddle. 'Light the candle!'

Twiddle lighted it – and at once Tinker jumped up on the bed in delight. Mrs Twiddle gave another squeal. 'What is it, what is it? Oh – it's *you*, Tinker! Twiddle, you bad, untruthful man, you said you'd put him into his kennel. How dare you tell me such a story!'

'Well, I *did* put him there,' said Mr Twiddle, feeling as if he were in some kind of peculiar dream. 'But I'm not going out to put him there again, wife. If there's a Tinker in the kennel and a Tinker here too, we've got two dogs, that's all. Good night!'

He went to sleep at once. Mrs Twiddle pushed Tinker off the bed, and went to sleep as well, very puzzled and very angry.

Tinker kept jumping up on top of her, and she dreamed of elephants sitting on her all night long. Poor Mrs Twiddle!

And in the morning, when Twiddle went to see if there *was* another Tinker in the kennel, he let out a very angry cat, who spat at him and scratched him, furious at having been shut up all the night long, when she badly wanted to hunt mice!

'It serves you right, Twiddle,' said his wife, when she saw the scratch. 'If you don't know the difference between the dog and the cat at night, it's just about time you learnt!'

9

Mr Twiddle and the cat

Mr Twiddle had a cold. He sneezed and snuffled, and Mrs Twiddle was very sorry for him.

'You shall have a hot drink,' she said, 'and I will buy you some nice lozenges to suck. Now, just sit by the fire, Twiddle, and keep warm.'

Twiddle sat by the fire, and toasted his legs and knees. The cat came up and purred. It loved a warm fire as much as Mr Twiddle did.

Puss jumped up on to Mr Twiddle's knee, and dug a claw into his trousers to hold on by. Twiddle gave a yell!

'Ow! You tiresome cat! You've pricked me with your claw. Get down! I've enough to do with warming myself without having you on my knee too!'

He pushed the cat down. Puss waited a few minutes till Mr Twiddle shut his eyes and nodded – and then up jumped Puss again. Mr Twiddle got a shock. His pipe fell out of his mouth, and broke on the hearth.

He was very angry. 'Look at that!' he said to the cat. 'Now look what you've done, you careless, stupid animal! You deserve to be smacked.'

Now the more Twiddle lost his temper with the cat, the more Puss seemed to want to come to him. It was most annoying. First the cat lay down on his feet, and he had to shuffle it off. Then it jumped up

on to the back of his chair and tried to lie round his neck. That made him very angry.

'Are you trying to be a scarf or something?' said Mr Twiddle to the cat. 'Get down! I don't want you on my feet and I don't want you round my neck. You are a real nuisance tonight. Do leave me alone.'

The cat disappeared. Mr Twiddle went to sleep. When he woke up he wanted to read the newspaper, so up he got to fetch it.

He didn't see the cat lying on the rug, curled up in a ball. He trod on it, fell flat on his nose, and the cat leapt up and scratched his cheek. Dear me, what an upset there was! Mr Twiddle yelled, the cat yowled and spat, and Mrs Twiddle came running in to see what the matter was.

'Twiddle, how dare you be unkind to the cat!' she cried. Twiddle got up and glared at her.

'You just scold the cat, not me,' he said. 'It's she who is being unkind to *me*! She won't leave me alone!'

He felt for his glasses. They had fallen off his nose. Mr Twiddle went down on his hands and knees to find them. He put his hand under the sofa, but the cat was hiding there, and thought he was playing. So she patted his fingers, and made him jump.

'If that cat isn't under the sofa now!' said Mr Twiddle. 'Wife, I tell you she won't leave me alone! Take her away. I can't bear any more tonight.'

Mrs Twiddle took the cat into the scullery and shut the door on her. The cat jumped up on to the table, found Mr Twiddle's supper there, ready for cooking, and ate it all up. Dear me, how angry he was when he heard about it!

'I'm going to bed,' he said. 'I can't stand that cat

any more. There's something strange about it tonight. It just won't leave me alone.'

'Don't be silly, Twiddle,' said his wife. She got up and went into the scullery. She filled a hot-water bottle and put a nice warm, furry cover on it. Then she went upstairs to put it into Twiddle's bed, whilst he went round the house and locked the doors.

Twiddle undressed. He grinned to himself when he thought of how he had shooed the cat out of the back door into the dark night. Now it wouldn't bother him any more. Ha ha! He wouldn't tell Mrs Twiddle. She would be cross if she knew the cat was out at night.

He threw back the sheets and jumped into bed. He put his feet down – and good gracious me, whatever was that in the bed? Twiddle gave a loud yell, jumped out again, and glared fearfully at the lump in the bed.

'That cat again!' he said. 'How did it get there? No sooner did I put my feet down than I felt it, all warm and furry. It's a magic cat tonight. What am I to do? I simply don't dare to get into bed. I shan't tell Mrs Twiddle. She will only laugh at me.'

Mrs Twiddle was sleeping in the spare-room bed that night, because she didn't want to catch Twiddle's cold. Her light was out. Twiddle stood in his bedroom and shivered.

'Fancy that tiresome cat thinking it would sleep in my bed!' he said to himself. 'Whatever next? And I shooed it out of the back door too! Well, I shall put on my dressing gown and spend the night in my chair in front of the kitchen fire. If that cat thinks it's going to bite my toes all night, it's mistaken!'

Poor Twiddle! He went downstairs to sit by the fire. He was almost asleep when Mrs Twiddle appeared, looking most surprised.

'Twiddle! Whatever are you doing? I looked in your room to see if you were all right, and you weren't there!'

'I couldn't get into bed,' said Twiddle sulkily. 'That cat was there.'

'Don't be silly, Twiddle. She never goes upstairs,' said Mrs Twiddle.

'I'm not silly,' said Twiddle. 'I tell you, that cat is lying in my bed, and I'm not going to sleep with it.'

Just then there came a mewing outside the back door, and something scratched and scraped at the door.

'But *that's* the cat!' cried Mrs Twiddle in surprise. 'I'd know her mew anywhere! However is it that she's outside, poor darling!'

'That's not the cat,' said Twiddle. 'I tell you, she's upstairs in my bed, as warm as a pie.'

Mrs Twiddle opened the back door – and in bounded the cat, purring with delight. She jumped straight on to Twiddle's knee. He gave a yell.

'Get off! Wife, there must be two cats then. I tell you one is asleep in my bed.'

'Well, we'll come and see,' said Mrs Twiddle, thinking that Twiddle must be quite mad. They went upstairs, and Mrs Twiddle threw back the covers. In the middle of the bed was the hot-water bottle she had put there, warm and cosy in its furry cover!

'You thought your hot-water bottle was the c-c-c-cat!' cried Mrs Twiddle, beginning to laugh and laugh. 'And you went downstairs in a rage, and left your lovely hot bottle to sleep in the bed by itself! Oh, Twiddle! Oh, Twiddle, you'll make me die of laughing one of these days!'

She laughed till she cried. Twiddle was angry and ashamed. He got into bed, put his feet on the hot bottle, and covered himself up.

'I'll have no more to do with that cat from now on,' he said. But, dear me, as soon as he was asleep, Puss jumped up on his bed and slept peacefully on Twiddle's feet all night long. Wouldn't Twiddle have been cross if he'd known!

10

Mr Twiddle and the dog

Once Mrs Twiddle looked after a friend's dog for a week. It was a nice little dog, called Scamp. It was most obedient, always wiped its paws on the mat when it came indoors, and said 'Wuff-wuff' for its food.

'Really, I'm quite sorry to part with the dog,' said Mrs Twiddle, patting it. 'Twiddle, will you take it back for me, please? My friend, Mrs Gubbins, would like to have it this morning.'

'Certainly, my dear, certainly!' said Mr Twiddle. 'Shall I go now? There's a bus I can catch in about ten minutes' time.'

'Yes – get your hat and go along,' said Mrs Twiddle. She gave the dog a biscuit, brushed his coat well, and fastened the lead to his collar.

'Dear, dear!' she said, feeling the collar. 'You must have grown fatter this week, Scamp. Your collar is too tight for your neck. I'll loosen it!'

She undid the collar and slipped the buckle along to another hole. The dog liked its collar loose. It knew it could slip it off then! It licked Mrs Twiddle's hands.

'Dear little thing,' said Mrs Twiddle. 'Now, Twiddle, hurry along or you'll miss that bus.'

Twiddle looked for his hat, put it on, and then, looking at his watch, he found that he only had about five minutes. He took hold of the lead and shot off

down the garden path, with the dog trotting after him. When he got to the gate Mr Twiddle found that he had forgotten to put his glasses on. He had cleaned them and left them on the table. Bother!

'Well, never mind, I shan't really need them,' said Mr Twiddle, hurrying along. 'I shall miss the bus if I don't walk fast.'

Now very soon the dog met a friend. This friend was a beautiful little Pekinese, and Scamp thought she was marvellous. The Pekinese wagged her feathery tail and Scamp wagged his.

'Stop a minute and talk to me,' said the Pekinese. So Scamp did a kind of double wriggle, and slipped his head neatly out of his loose collar. He wagged his tail at the Pekinese, and joyfully licked her nose. He was ready for a jolly good game!

The Pekinese looked after Mr Twiddle in astonishment. 'Does he mind going without you?' she asked.

'I haven't asked him,' said Scamp. 'I say, doesn't my collar look funny running along the road without me, on the end of the lead! What will Twiddle say when he sees it?'

With a bound Scamp ran round the corner and began to have a fine game with his little friend. Mr Twiddle didn't even see him go. He trotted along down the street, pulling the lead and empty collar behind him, whistling a little tune, and keeping a sharp lookout for the bus at the corner.

He met his friend, Mr Jinks, who stared in astonishment at the sight of Twiddle hurrying along pulling a collar behind him.

'Where are you going?' he called.

'Just taking this dear little dog back to its owner,' said Twiddle, beaming. 'Isn't it a good little soul, trotting along behind me so happily?'

Mr Jinks thought that Mr Twiddle must be a little mad that morning. But there wasn't any time to say so, because Twiddle hurried on so quickly. Mr Jinks stared at the collar running along behind Mr Twiddle, and began to laugh.

Mr Twiddle got to the corner just at the same moment as the bus did. He jumped up, and pulled the lead and collar behind him.

'Now just go under the seat and lie down quietly,' said Mr Twiddle, peering round for Scamp. He couldn't see him, so he thought he must have gone under the seat already.

'Good dog,' he said to the empty collar there. 'Very good dog! Conductor, I want a twopenny ticket for myself, and a ticket for my dog.'

'What dog?' asked the conductor in amazement.

'The dog with me, of course,' said Mr Twiddle.

'Really, some people do ask silly questions. Don't you know a dog when you see one? Perhaps you thought I had a cat or a canary on my lead.'

The conductor looked offended. He thought that if Mr Twiddle really wanted to buy a ticket for a dog that wasn't there, he might as well let him. So he gave him a twopenny ticket and a dog's ticket as well.

A very big lady got in with a small dog under her arm. She tried to sit down beside Mr Twiddle.

'Madam, I have a dog under my seat,' said Mr Twiddle. 'Perhaps it would be better if you took the seat over there. Our two dogs might fight.'

The big lady looked under the seat and saw no dog at all. Only an empty collar. She thought it was a trick to make her take another seat and leave Mr Twiddle comfortably alone in his.

So she sat down opposite to him and glared at him with large black eyes. Mr Twiddle felt most uncomfortable.

'I suppose you think you are very clever,' said the big lady in a freezing sort of voice.

Mr Twiddle was astonished. He had never thought himself clever, to begin with – and he couldn't imagine why the big lady should think he did. He felt more and more uncomfortable as he sat under the glare of the lady's big black eyes, and he bent down and spoke to Scamp, whom he still thought was lying quietly under the seat.

It was dark under the seat, and Mr Twiddle hadn't got his glasses, so he couldn't see a thing. He spoke in a quiet voice.

'Good dog, Scamp. Very good dog. Lie down quietly now.'

Not a sound came from under the seat, which wasn't at all surprising.

'You do think you're funny, don't you?' said the big lady in a scornful sort of voice.

'Well, Madam, no, I can't say that I have ever thought myself funny,' said Twiddle. He got up to go, because he couldn't bear to think what the strange big lady would say next. 'Come on, Scamp!' he said. 'Come on.'

'Mind he doesn't bite you!' called the big lady after him. Twiddle thought that was a silly remark. He jumped off the bus, and with his nose well up in the air he hurried along.

'Hie! Your dog's gone to chase a cat!' a boy shouted after him.

'Silly child!' thought Twiddle, pulling the lead behind him. 'Thinks he'll make me look behind and see if Scamp really has gone chasing cats. Well, I won't!'

'Hie! Your dog's lost!' yelled another boy.

'Dear me, I wonder why children are so stupid this

morning,' thought poor Twiddle. 'Ah – here is Mrs Gubbins's house!'

He went up the path and knocked at the door. Mrs Gubbins opened it.

'Oh, do come in,' she said. 'I wondered if you'd bring back my darling Scamp today!'

'Then you wondered right,' said Twiddle happily, pulling the collar behind him in the hall. 'I've brought him – and he's been as good as gold all the time!'

He looked round to see Scamp, but the hall was dark, and he could see nothing. 'He must have gone under the chest there!' he said. 'Scamp! Scamp!'

'But he didn't come in with you,' said Mrs Gubbins, puzzled. 'At least, *I* never saw him!'

'He was just at my heels,' said Mr Twiddle. 'I had him on the lead.'

He pulled at the lead – and the empty collar slid over the floor to Mr Twiddle's foot. Mr Twiddle bent down to pat the dog that wasn't there. His hand found the empty collar and he picked it up and blinked at it.

'Good gracious!' he said. 'He's slipped his collar, the rascal. Well, I'm sure he's under the chest, Mrs Gubbins. You call him and see. I must go now or I'll miss the bus back. Goodbye, Scamp, dear little chap! Goodbye!'

He trotted off down the path again to the bus, whilst Mrs Gubbins looked all about for a dog she couldn't find. Twiddle caught the bus and was soon trotting home down the street.

'Well!' cried Mrs Twiddle, opening the door to him, 'and where have *you* been all this time? Didn't I tell you to take Scamp back to Mrs Gubbins for me?'

'Well, my dear, I did,' said Twiddle, in surprise. 'He was as good as gold all the way, and I left him safely under the chest in the hall at Mrs Gubbins's.'

'Oh – and I suppose he caught the bus back, and arrived home before you did,' said Mrs Twiddle, in a rage. 'Scamp! Come here!'

And to poor Twiddle's enormous astonishment Scamp came rushing out of the kitchen, put his front paws on Twiddle's middle, and tried to reach up and lick him.

'But I've just taken you to your mistress!' cried Twiddle, sitting down in alarm. 'Wife, there must be two Scamps. There really must.'

'Well, it's a good thing there's not two Twiddles!' said Mrs Twiddle with a snort. 'Now *I* shall have to take Scamp home myself – and without a collar and lead too. Really, Twiddle, I've a good mind to BOX YOUR EARS.'

She looked so fierce that poor Twiddle ran out to the garden shed and sat there the rest of the day. And he still cannot think how it was that he took Scamp home – and yet found him waiting for him when he came back!

11

Mr Twiddle's spectacles

'Have you seen my spectacles, Mrs Twiddle?' asked Mr Twiddle, looking all round for them.

'Oh, dear! Have you lost them *again*?' sighed Mrs Twiddle. 'I'm getting so tired of it, Twiddle. Twenty times a day you say the same thing to me – "Have you seen my spectacles?" Why don't you keep them in the same place, whenever you take them off, then you would know where they were.'

'That's a good idea,' said Mr Twiddle, blinking all round the room to see if he could find them. 'But what is a safe place? Wherever I put them, they seem to disappear at once.'

'Oh no they don't,' said Mrs Twiddle. 'You just put them down anywhere and forget them – then you look for them in the wrong place and say they've gone. Why, I found them inside the teapot yesterday, Twiddle. Whatever made you put them there?'

'Dear me, were they really there?' said Twiddle. 'Well, I wonder if they are there now.'

But they weren't. Twiddle looked round everywhere, but his glasses really did seem to have vanished this time.

'When did you last take them off?' asked Mrs Twiddle, knitting away hard.

'Let me see now – oh yes, I took them off in the bathroom when I went to wash my face,' said Mr Twiddle. 'Yes, I distinctly remember doing that.'

'Well, you have probably put your spectacles in the bath then, if I know anything about you,' said Mrs Twiddle. 'You had better go and look.'

Mr Twiddle went – and he came back looking rather foolish. He had his glasses on his nose.

'You were quite right, my dear,' he said to Mrs Twiddle. 'I *had* put them into the bath. I suppose I thought they would be safe there whilst I washed. And, of course, I left them there by mistake.'

'Now listen to me, Twiddle,' said Mrs Twiddle. 'You just think of some really good place to put your glasses whenever you take them off – and *always* put them there – and then you will never, never have to look for them. You will always know exactly where they are.'

'That *is* a good idea, Wife,' said Twiddle, pleased. 'Now where would be a good place? On top of the clock, do you think?'

'And do you think you could easily get them off the clock if you are out to tea?' said Mrs Twiddle. 'Or suppose you are at the bottom of the garden – will you like coming all the way into the house to fetch them? No – you won't. Now be sensible, Twiddle, and think of some safe place that is easy to get at wherever you are.'

Mrs Twiddle heard the back door bell and she got up to answer it. Twiddle stood and thought about his glasses. Where would be the best place to keep them? He thought and thought – and then he smiled.

'*I* know a good place!' he said. 'I'll put them into their brown leather case – and slip the case into one of my socks! Then whenever I want my glasses, all I shall have to do will be to bend down and slip the case out of my sock. Ah, that *is* a good place, to be sure!'

He put his glasses into their case, bent down and pulled up his trouser leg – and slipped the fat brown case into the top of his sock. The suspender kept it tight. His glasses would be quite safe there. Really, that was a very clever idea.

Mrs Twiddle called to him. 'Twiddle! The fish hasn't come yet! I must go out and get it. I shan't be long.'

'Very well, dear,' called back Mr Twiddle. 'I'll answer the bells whilst you are gone.'

Mrs Twiddle went out. Mr Twiddle made up the kitchen fire. He shooed the cat away from the larder. He cleaned his shoes slowly till they shone like black polished wood. And then he felt that he really did deserve a sit-down!

So down he sat in his armchair. He took up the paper and began to read – but, dear me, he couldn't see to read without his glasses! So he looked on the table for them.

They were not there, of course. They were in his left sock. But dear old Twiddle had forgotten all about that. He got up and looked in his chair seat. Sometimes he left his glasses there. But no, they were not there this time.

'Dear, dear! Gone again!' said Mr Twiddle, really cross. 'Now how am I to read without my glasses?'

He hunted all round the kitchen. He hunted all over the bedroom. He hunted everywhere – except in his left sock! Then he wondered what Mrs Twiddle would say if she came home and found him hunting for his glasses again.

'I am sure I must have dropped them out-of-doors somewhere,' said Twiddle. 'I've looked simply everywhere *in*doors. Yes – I must have dropped them in the road. Dear, dear – what a sad thing! I must put a notice in the paper to say I will give a reward to anyone finding them.'

Mrs Twiddle came back at that minute and Twiddle called to her, 'I'm just going out for a minute, dear. I won't be long.'

So out he went to the newspaper office. The man there said yes, he could put a notice into the paper about Mr Twiddle's glasses. He pushed a sheet of notepaper over to him.

'Just write down what you want us to put into the paper,' he said. 'What sort of glasses they are, and so on.'

Mr Twiddle took the paper and a pen. He stood and thought. Yes – he knew what to say. He would say 'LOST – a nice pair of tortoiseshell glasses. Finder will be given half a crown.'

He began to write the notice down – but he couldn't very well see without his glasses. He fumbled about for them in his pocket. Then he beamed. Of course – they were in his sock. He bent down, turned up his trouser leg, and took out his spectacle case from his sock.

He put the case on the table and opened it. He took out his spectacles and put them on his nose. Then he noticed that the man was staring at him very hard.

'Staring is rude,' said Mr Twiddle. 'Is anything wrong with me?'

'No,' said the man, and he giggled.

'What's the joke?' asked Mr Twiddle crossly. 'Am I the joke?'

'Well – yes, in a way,' said the man. 'Write out the notice, please, sir.'

Grumbling away to himself, Mr Twiddle wrote out his notice. Then he gave it to the man, who read it and chuckled. He looked at Mr Twiddle and held out his hand.

'Half a crown, please, sir,' he said. 'I've found your glasses for you.'

'No, really!' cried Twiddle, excited. 'Where did you find them? Do tell me!'

'Here they are,' said the man, and he neatly took them off Twiddle's nose, put them into his case, and handed them to Twiddle. 'Half a crown, reward, please.'

'B-b-b-b-b-but,' stammered Twiddle. 'B-b-but – how did they get there?'

'Well, you took them out of your sock and put them on your nose yourself,' said the man, giggling. 'Now, Mr Twiddle, pay up. It would cost you three shillings to put that notice into the paper – but it will only cost you half a crown reward. I did find them, didn't I – on your nose!'

Mr Twiddle paid half a crown in disgust. How could he be so silly as to offer a reward to anyone finding his glasses when they were on his nose all the time!

He went home and told Mrs Twiddle all about it. 'And where are your glasses now?' asked Mrs Twiddle, seeing that they were not on his nose.

'I expect they are in my sock,' said Mr Twiddle, and he bent down to look. But, you know, they were *not* there! Mr Twiddle scratched his head and frowned.

'Oh dear!' he said. 'Oh dear – I must have left them on the table at the paper office. Yes – that man must have got them there. Dear, dear, dear – I hope I shan't have to pay him another half-crown for finding them!'

Off he went to get them. Really, it's a wonder he ever has them at all, isn't it!

12

Mr Twiddle goes out at night

One night Mr and Mrs Twiddle were asked to go to Mr Fankle's birthday party.

'Mr Fankle doesn't get home till seven o'clock,' said Mrs Fankle, 'so it will have to be a supper party. Can you come?'

'We'd love to,' said Mrs Twiddle. 'Only it is so dreadfully dark at night now, with no streetlamps. Still, we have our torches, and we'll come along, Mrs Fankle. Thank you for the invitation.'

'I know!' cried Mrs Fankle suddenly. '*You* come along to tea with me in the afternoon, Mrs Twiddle, and help me to get the supper things ready. Then you won't need to come here in the dark. Twiddle can come along by himself quite easily, can't he?'

'Oh yes,' said Mrs Twiddle. 'I'll leave all his things ready for him, and he can dress himself and come along at eight o'clock.'

So, on the day of Mr Fankle's party, Mrs Twiddle called to Mr Twiddle.

'Twiddle! I am leaving all your things ready for you here!' she cried. 'There is your evening cloak – your top hat – your best white handkerchief – your stick – and a parcel in which I've put your present for Mr Fankle.'

'Yes, dear,' said Mr Twiddle, not really paying much attention. 'Yes, dear. I'll remember, dear.'

Now Mrs Twiddle was calling from his bedroom, where she had laid out all the things for Mr Twiddle. But, Twiddle thought she was calling from the kitchen, and so, that night, when he wanted to go to the party, he walked out to the kitchen to get ready.

There was nobody there. Mr Twiddle did not dare to light a candle, because Mrs Twiddle had not drawn the curtains before she had left that afternoon, and Mr Twiddle knew that his wife would not have a light on unless the window was covered.

So he began to feel about for his things. Of course they were not there – they were up in his bedroom; but Mr Twiddle didn't think of that. He wandered round the dark kitchen, feeling here and there for his things – but, dear me! he couldn't seem to find them at all!

'Where *has* Mrs Twiddle put them?' he said crossly. 'Really, she's a very silly woman. Why didn't she put them on the table, where I could easily get them? And why didn't she draw the curtains before she went so that I could light a candle and see what I am doing?'

Mr Twiddle didn't think of drawing the curtains himself. He just went on looking and looking. He brushed against the table, and the cloth fell on the floor. When Mr Twiddle went walking round that side of the table again, he stumbled over the cloth.

'Ah! There's my cloak!' he said, and bent to pick it up. 'Fancy Mrs Twiddle putting it on the floor. Silly woman!'

He tried his best to put the tablecloth on like a cloak, but he couldn't. So he just wrapped it somehow round himself, and then felt about for his hat.

'That may be on the floor too,' said Mr Twiddle. 'If Mrs Twiddle put my cloak on the floor, I expect she will have put my hat there too. Dear, dear, dear!'

So he felt round the floor, and came to the waste-paper basket. It was round and tall, and felt to Mr Twiddle just like his hat. He picked it up and put it on. Luckily it was empty.

'Seems a bit tight for me,' said Mr Twiddle, puzzled. 'My head must have grown! Well, well! never mind, that's my hat found. Now for my white handkerchief.'

He found a duster on the dresser, and stuffed that into his pocket, leaving a little bit of yellow hanging out. Then he hunted for his stick.

He found the poker, though he thought it felt rather heavier than usual for a stick. However, he tucked it under his arm, and was just about to go when he remembered the parcel for Mr Fankle's birthday.

'Gracious! I nearly forgot it!' he said, and began to hunt around again for a parcel. He soon found one, though he didn't know it was only Mrs Twiddle's old boots wrapped up to give away to the charwoman. He put it under his arm and set off, banging the door behind him.

He wore the bright red kitchen tablecloth round his shoulders, the wastepaper basket for a hat; he had a yellow duster in his pocket instead of a handkerchief, and he carried the kitchen poker for his stick. Really, Mr Twiddle!

He knocked at Mr Fankle's door. He was late, and everyone else had arrived.

'That must be Mr Twiddle!' cried Mrs Fankle, and she ran to the door to open it, followed by all the others. Twiddle stepped inside. The door shut, and Mrs Fankle switched on the light.

And then there was an astonished silence, as everyone looked at Mr Twiddle. *How* peculiar he looked!

'Well, what's the matter?' asked Mr Twiddle, puzzled.

'Er – have you come in fancy dress?' asked Mr Fankle, trying not to laugh.

'Of course not,' said Mr Twiddle crossly. And then he stared at the wastepaper basket he had taken off his head. He looked at the red kitchen cloth – and the poker. He went very red.

'Twiddle!' cried Mrs Twiddle. 'Whatever have you dressed yourself up like that for? You *do* look silly!'

'It was a mistake,' said Twiddle, putting down the basket, and taking off the red cloth. He stood the poker in the umbrella stand, and tried to look merry and bright. He felt hot and bothered, so he took out his handkerchief to mop his head – and pulled out the yellow kitchen duster!

'Twiddle!' squealed Mrs Twiddle. 'My duster! What did you take that for?'

Twiddle threw the duster down in a temper. Then he gave the parcel to Mr Fankle.

'Many happy returns of the day,' he said. 'Here is a little present for you.'

'Oh, thank you,' said Mr Fankle, and undid the parcel. Out fell Mrs Twiddle's holey old boots!

'Well, really, what a funny present!' said Mr Fankle, puzzled. Mrs Twiddle began to laugh.

'Oh, he's brought the wrong parcel!' she said. 'I know what he's done, the silly man! He looked for his things in the dark kitchen instead of upstairs in the bedroom where there is a light and where I had put out all his clothes, *and* the right parcel! Oh, Twiddle! Oh, Twiddle! I shall die of laughing, I know I shall!'

And she began to laugh and laugh and laugh. Everyone else laughed too – really, what *would* old Twiddle do next? Who would have thought anyone would have worn a wastepaper basket for a hat and the kitchen tablecloth for a cloak!

Twiddle stood there looking sulky and red – and then *he* suddenly began to laugh too. You should have heard him – ha, ha, ha! ho, ho, ho! he, he, he!

'Yes,' he said, wiping his eyes, 'I'm a silly fellow – but anyway, I've given you a good joke for your birthday, Mr Fankle!' And he certainly had!

13

Mr Twiddle is a funny fellow

One morning Mrs Twiddle wanted to make some buns and she found that she had no eggs.

'Twiddle!' she cried. 'Where are you? Oh, there you are, asleep in a deck chair in the sun as usual! Get up, lazybones, and go and do a little shopping for me.'

'I wasn't asleep, my dear – I only just shut my eyes because the sun was rather bright,' said Mr Twiddle, getting up at once.

'Well, if you were awake, it's funny you should snore,' said Mrs Twiddle. 'Now, Twiddle, take my basket – it's over there. And go to the grocer's, and ask for three eggs, a small bag of flour, and a pound of currants. Hurry now, because my oven is getting nice and hot for the buns.'

Twiddle took the basket and hurried. He ran down the road to the grocer's. He asked for a bag of flour, which the grocer gave him. A pound of currants, and he got those too. But when he asked for three eggs, the grocer shook his head.

'Sorry, sir,' he said, 'but I've no eggs today. I may have some tomorrow.'

'But Mrs Twiddle will be very cross with me if I go home without eggs,' said Twiddle in dismay. 'You see she wants to make buns, and her oven is getting hot.'

'That's a pity,' said the grocer. 'Well, look, Mr Twiddle, sir – take some egg powder instead. It will do quite well in place of eggs.'

'All right, I will,' said Twiddle. The grocer shook some yellow egg powder into a paper, twisted it up, and gave it to Twiddle. He paid the bill, put the things into his basket, and set out again for home.

He bought some tobacco for himself, and a paper, and then stood for a moment at the gate of a field. It was full of golden buttercups, and looked very lovely.

'I think I will walk home through the fields,' said Mr Twiddle to himself. 'It will do me good. And those buttercups are beautiful to see.'

So off he went through the buttercup fields. His legs brushed against hundreds of golden buttercup heads, and they shook their yellow pollen against his trousers. And when dear old Twiddle came out into the road again he found that his trouser legs were covered with yellow powder!

'Goodness gracious! Look at that! What can it be? It's something that has fallen out of the bottom of my basket!' said Twiddle in dismay. He stared at his basket, and remembered what he had in it.

'Yes – it must be the egg powder! It was bright yellow, I remember. The grocer must have twisted up the packet so loosely that all the powder has dribbled out of it, through the bottom of my basket and down my trouser legs,' said Twiddle. He felt rather clever to have thought all this out.

He scratched his head and thought hard again.

'I must go back and get some more. It's no good going home with an empty packet, and Mrs Twiddle asking for eggs,' he said to himself.

So back he went to the grocer's. 'I'm sorry,' said Mr Twiddle, 'but all the egg powder has fallen out of the packet down my trousers. Look at it! I must have some more.'

'You must have put it rather carelessly into your basket,' said the grocer. He brushed all the yellow powder from Twiddle's trousers and gave him another packet, very firmly twisted up indeed. Twiddle carefully poked it down into his basket and set off again. He thought he would have time to walk through the fields again. It had been so very pleasant last time.

'The buttercups are like a big golden carpet spread out for a king to tread upon,' said Twiddle to himself, and he pretended that he was the king, and walked on very haughtily, his head in the air.

And, of course, when he came out into the road again, what did he see but yellow powder all over his trouser legs once more!

'Well, really, this is very vexing!' said Twiddle, annoyed. 'The second lot of egg powder has shaken out of the basket too! That grocer *does* pack his things carelessly.'

So back he ran to the grocer's again, feeling hot and out of breath. He banged his basket down on the floor. 'Look at my trouser legs again!' he cried. 'That egg powder of yours has shaken loose from the package once more! I've lost it all! Get me some more, please, and put it into a tight-lidded box this time!'

The grocer was busy and cross. He told his boy to give the powder to Twiddle in a box with a very tight-fitting lid.

The boy put it into the basket, and Twiddle marched off for the third time. He looked at his watch and decided that he hadn't time to go through the fields again. He had better run all the way down the road!

So he set off, and arrived home very hot and panting indeed.

'What a long time you've been!' cried Mrs Twiddle. 'Here I've been waiting and waiting for those things, and my oven's so hot now that it would roast a large turkey!'

Twiddle put the basket on the table and wiped his forehead. 'Now I'll just tell you what's happened,' he began. 'It was most annoying. . . .'

'Oh, I haven't time to hear your excuses!' cried Mrs Twiddle. 'Did you bring the eggs?'

'No,' said Twiddle. 'There are no eggs today. So I brought egg powder instead. And just let me tell you about that – the grocer was very foolish and. . . .'

'Go into the garden, Twiddle!' cried Mrs Twiddle, who was anxious to get on with her cake-making. 'I'll listen to you after I've done my baking!'

Twiddle was cross. He went into the garden and sank into his deck chair with his pipe and paper. But he was so tired that he fell fast asleep.

But not for long! Out came Mrs Twiddle, carrying two packets and a box, and looking very puzzled indeed.

'Twiddle! Twiddle!' she cried. 'You must really be quite mad! You have brought back two packets of egg powder and a boxful too! I shan't want so much. It is most extravagant of you!'

Twiddle woke with a jump. He stared at the two packets and the box. They were all quite full of egg powder, fine and yellow. He stared at the yellow powder on his trousers, and he thought he must be dreaming.

'It's all right,' he told his wife. 'I'm just dreaming this. I couldn't spill two packets of egg powder down my trousers, and still bring two full packets home and a box too. So I must be dreaming. Don't worry about it. I shall wake up in a minute, and then you will see that the two packets are empty, not full.'

'Twiddle! Don't be so silly!' cried Mrs Twiddle, most annoyed. 'You may be asleep and dreaming, but I most certainly am not! I tell you there are three

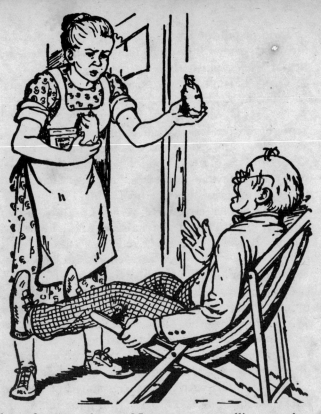

lots of egg powder, and I INSIST on you telling me why you brought three instead of one.'

Well, of course, that was just what poor old Twiddle couldn't do. He stared at the egg powder in the packets, and he stared at the powder on his trouser legs, and he never once thought it was buttercup pollen. So how could he explain anything to Mrs Twiddle?

She was cross. He was upset. And the buns burnt in the hot oven. So altogether it was a most unlucky day, and only the buttercups that nodded their heads in the summer breeze knew the meaning of the puzzle!

14

Mr Twiddle tries to help

Once Mrs Twiddle twisted her ankle and couldn't get about as usual to do her work. Mr Twiddle was very sorry for her.

'Now, my dear, you just sit down and let me run about for you!' he said. 'I've got a pair of legs, haven't I? Well, I can do everything just as well as you!'

'You want brains as well as legs, dear Twiddle,' said Mrs Twiddle, sitting down with a sigh. 'Oh, my poor ankle! Well well – you must do a little to help me, Twiddle, that's quite certain.'

Twiddle worked quite well for a while. He wrote out the list for the washing. He dusted the drawing room. He fed the cat. Then he felt really tired and he sat down to have a rest.

Mrs Twiddle called to him. 'Twiddle! Twiddle! Where have you got to? There's somebody at the back door. And did you put the pudding in the oven as I told you to?'

Twiddle was half asleep. He got up at once, and, rubbing his eyes, he went to the back door. A boy was there with a clock.

'Your clock's mended, sir,' said the boy, and gave Mr Twiddle his lovely drawing-room clock. Mr Twiddle was pleased. He had missed the clock, because it struck the half-hours and chimed the hours. It was a nice clock.

'It's the clock come back,' he said to Mrs Twiddle. 'I must just put it on the drawing-room mantelpiece.'

'Oh, Twiddle, I do wish you'd put the rice pudding into the oven first,' said Mrs Twiddle. 'I keep asking you to. It won't be ready by dinner time if you don't. Do do as you are told, if you really want to help me!'

'All right, all right, my dear,' said Twiddle, still half asleep. And whatever *do* you think he did?

Why, he put the drawing-room clock into the oven and then picked up the rice pudding in its enamel dish and put it carefully on the drawing-room mantelpiece!

He just wasn't thinking what he was doing, of course. He shut the oven door on the clock and then went to see what else he could do.

Mrs Twiddle hadn't noticed anything. She was knitting hard. The cat gave a mew when it saw the pudding in the middle of the drawing-room mantel-piece, but nobody took any notice of the mew. So the cat settled down and went to sleep.

After a bit the clock in the oven struck the half-hour. Mrs Twiddle looked up.

'Why, Twiddle,' she said, 'that clock is some-where in the kitchen! I distinctly heard it strike.'

'How can it strike in the kitchen when I put it in the drawing room?' asked Twiddle, feeling cross. 'You do say surprising things, Wife.'

'Well, I suppose I was mistaken,' said Mrs Twiddle, knitting again.

Now, at twelve o'clock, the clock not only struck twelve times, but chimed too!

Ding, dong, ding, dong! it went; ding, dong, ding, dong!

'Twiddle! That clock is *cer*tainly in the kitchen!' said Mrs Twiddle.

Well, Twiddle had heard it strike and chime as well, and he too felt sure it was in the kitchen. So he looked round, but he couldn't see it anywhere, of course. This wasn't surprising, as it was still in the oven.

'I can't understand it, Wife,' said Twiddle, scratching his head. 'I distinctly remember taking it into the drawing room.'

'Twiddle, just look and see if the milk pudding is getting on all right,' said Mrs Twiddle. 'It should be doing nicely now.'

Twiddle opened the oven door – and inside was the drawing-room clock, looking out at him with a very surprised face, because it was slowly cooking and didn't like it at all!

'*Twiddle!* You surely didn't put the clock to cook in the oven!' cried Mrs Twiddle. 'Oh, Twiddle – and we've just had it mended. Oh, I'm sure it will have done it no good to cook like that. You foolish man! Take it out at once!'

So Twiddle, looking very foolish, took it out and set it on the shelf to cool. It made a very peculiar noise and then stopped ticking.

'It's stopped!' said Mrs Twiddle. 'Now it will have to go and be mended again – and it's only just come back! Really, Twiddle! And what about the pudding? Did you look in the oven and see how that is doing?'

Twiddle looked – but of course the pudding wasn't there. It was most extraordinary. 'I know I *put* it there!' said Twiddle. 'I feel sure I did. But it's vanished.'

Just then there came a knock at the front door. 'There's Mrs Harris,' said Mrs Twiddle. 'Show her into the drawing room, please, Twiddle, and say I will come in half a minute. I must just put my shoe on.'

Twiddle went to the front door and showed Mrs Harris into the drawing room. He said that Mrs Twiddle would only be a minute. And it wasn't long before his wife was hobbling into the drawing room with a stick.

'Good morning, Mrs Twiddle,' said Mrs Harris. 'Did you know that your cat was eating an uncooked rice pudding in the middle of the mantelpiece? I just wondered if that was the usual place to give her her dinner.'

Mrs Twiddle looked at the mantelpiece in horror – and sure enough there was Puss lapping up the milk and the rice for all she was worth, enjoying such an unusual treat!

'Shoo, Puss, shoo!' cried Mrs Twiddle, clapping her hands at once. The cat leapt off and upset the dish. The milk dripped into the fender and the dish fell with a clatter.

'Twiddle! Twiddle! You put the pudding on the mantelpiece instead of the clock, and you put the clock in the oven instead of the pudding!' cried Mrs Twiddle. 'Oh, it's much quicker to do things

myself! What a stupid, foolish man you are, to be sure!'

And poor Twiddle thought the same as he fetched a cloth to mop up the milky mess. 'I've got to pay to mend the clock again,' he thought sadly. 'And I've spoilt the pudding. But never mind about that! I never *did* like rice puddings!'

Whatever will he do next? I really can't think!

2. WELL, REALLY, MR TWIDDLE!

A Beaver Book
Published by Arrow Books Limited
62–5 Chandos Place, London WC2N 4NW

An imprint of Century Hutchinson Ltd

London Melbourne Sydney Auckland
Johannesburg and agencies throughout
the world

First published in 1953
Revised edition published in 1968 by
Dean and Son Limited
Beaver edition 1982
Reprinted 1984 and 1989

Printed and bound in Great Britain by
Cox & Wyman Ltd, Reading

ISBN 0 09 965560 8

Contents

1

Well, really, Mr Twiddle!

'I'm certainly in luck today, wife,' said Mr Twiddle, looking very pleased with himself. 'First, I found that nice pencil I lost last week, and then when I went to feed the hens there were five eggs, and now the postman has brought me a present from my sister Hannah – a nice new hat!'

He tried it on. It certainly was a nice hat. Mrs Twiddle wanted to put a little brown hen feather in the band, but Mr Twiddle wouldn't let her.

'No. I don't like feathers in hats,' he said. 'If only I had a nice new suit now, to go with my hat. I *should* look smart!'

'Well, as you're having such a lucky day you might find one lying in the road,' said Mrs Twiddle, with a giggle.

'You simply never know what might happen when your luck is in,' said Twiddle. 'I wouldn't be a bit surprised if I found a five-pound note when I was out walking this morning.'

'Well, you'd have to take it to the police station and hand it in to the police, and tell them to find the owner,' said Mrs Twiddle.

'Ah, but as my luck is in they wouldn't find the owner, and they would have to give it back to me,' said Mr Twiddle, still admiring himself in his new hat.

'You've got it on back to front, but I suppose you

don't really mind that,' said Mrs Twiddle, with another little giggle.

A timid knock came at the door, and a little girl's head peeped in. 'Please, Mrs Twiddle, may I borrow your cat to play with this morning?'

'Certainly, dear,' said Mrs Twiddle. 'Call her. She does so love playing with a kind little girl like you.'

Mr Twiddle watched the little girl carry the purring cat away, and he looked very pleased. 'Well, if that isn't *another* bit of luck!' he said. 'We've got rid of that cat for a whole morning. Now I can walk about the house without falling over it.'

'I don't know why you don't like our dear old cat,' said Mrs Twiddle. 'You're the only person who ever falls over it, anyway.'

'And do you know why?' said Mr Twiddle, suddenly looking rather fierce. 'I'll tell you! It's because I'm the only person that cat tries to trip up! She's

always walking through my legs! Bit of good luck, I tell you, Puss going off with Polly.'

'Well, if you don't go and get the fish for dinner your good luck will come to an end, because you'll go hungry,' said Mrs Twiddle, looking at the clock. 'Put on your old hat, Twiddle, and get the shopping basket, do. Take some paper with you for the fish.'

Twiddle fetched the basket. He put a newspaper in it to wrap the fish in when he bought it. But he didn't change his nice new hat for his old one. No, he thought he looked so nice in the new one that he felt he might as well give everyone a treat when they looked at him!

'Put your *old* hat on!' called Mrs Twiddle, when she saw him going out with his new one on his head.

'No, no, dear,' said Mr Twiddle, trying to find a quick reason for keeping it on. 'I told you my luck is in today – suppose I find a nice new suit somewhere. I'd look dreadful if I didn't have a nice hat to wear with it.'

'Don't be silly, Twiddle!' called his wife, but by that time he was out of the front gate and couldn't hear her. He hurried along to the fish shop.

He stood in the queue for ten minutes and then got a large piece of rather smelly cod. He had it wrapped carefully in the newspaper, and hoped that he wouldn't be followed home by half a dozen cats.

'I won't go home through the village in case the cats smell the fish and come after me,' thought Twiddle, remembering how annoyed he had been last time by having five cats trailing after him all the way home, sniffing the kippers in his basket. 'I'll go back through the wood.'

So he took the other way home and wandered along in the wood, enjoying the smell of the hawthorn blossom and the sight of the bluebells. It was a very hot day, and Mr Twiddle was glad he hadn't got an overcoat on.

Then he saw a most extraordinary sight. He stopped and looked as if he couldn't believe his eyes. Neatly folded up under a bush was a suit of beautiful new clothes!

Twiddle stood and stared and his heart began to thump in excitement. There! What had he said that very morning! His luck was certainly in, because here was a new suit of clothes waiting to go with his nice new hat!

'But, wait, Twiddle,' said Twiddle to himself, cautiously. 'They might belong to someone, you know. Have a look around and see.'

So he had a good look round, but he could see nobody at all. He went back to the neat pile of clothes and looked at them. Coat, trousers, waistcoat, vest, socks, braces . . . why, there was everything except a hat!

'This is most extraordinary,' said Twiddle. 'It just shows what can happen when your luck is in! I get a new hat from Hannah – and, lo and behold, I find a complete set of new clothes to go with it, and nobody to own them!'

He looked at them again. They were exactly his size. They were *meant* for him! He looked at the collar of the suit, half expecting to see his own name marked there, and was quite disappointed when it wasn't. But, would you believe it, on the neat white handkerchief folded inside the left-hand top pocket of the coat was the letter T in pale blue thread! Twiddle stared in the greatest delight.

'That proves it,' he said. 'Absolutely. Completely. No doubt whatever. This certainly is my lucky morning! Goodness knows what I shall find next!'

He picked up the clothes and was about to put

them into his basket when he remembered the fish. 'Better undo the fish, take a bit of the paper and wrap up the clothes in it or they'll smell of fish,' said Twiddle, forgetting that the paper must smell very strongly of fish already.

He wrapped the clothes up carefully in some of the newspaper, and then made his way home, wondering what bit of good luck would happen to him next. 'I shall put on this new suit as soon as I get home,' thought Mr Twiddle, 'and wear it with my new hat. How grand I shall look!'

He was longing to tell his wife of his new piece of luck, and he was disappointed when he got home and found that she was out. He went to get himself some lemonade to drink, and then heard Mrs Twiddle at the front door. She was talking to somebody.

'Bother! She's brought a visitor home,' thought Mr Twiddle, who didn't like his wife's visitors very much because they talked such a lot.

Then he got a terrible shock. Mrs Twiddle brought her visitor into the kitchen, and Twiddle could hardly believe his eyes when he saw a poor, shivering, dripping man in a wet bathing suit! He gaped at him in surprise.

'Twiddle! I met this poor fellow running down the street in an awful state,' said Mrs Twiddle. 'He thought he would bathe in the Blue Pool because it was so hot today, so he took his bathing suit and went to the wood. He took off his nice new clothes, hid them under a bush, and went to bathe.'

'And w-w-when I c-c-c-came b-b-b-back, they had been t-t-taken by a r-r-robber!' said the shivering man, standing as close to the kitchen fire as he could.

'So, Twiddle, I bought the poor fellow in here, and I thought you could lend him a suit,' said Mrs

Twiddle, 'and I thought I'd give him a good hot meal, or he'll get a terrible cold, and then perhaps you'd go along to the police station with him and tell the police about the robbery. I mean, a man who is hateful enough to take a bather's clothes deserves to go to prison at once!'

Twiddle's heart went right down into his boots and stayed there. He stared at his wife in such a peculiar way that she thought he must be ill. He couldn't say a single word.

But he thought a lot! 'Oh, dear! So they were *his* clothes – and he was bathing! Why didn't I think of the Blue Pool? Oh dear, oh dear – I hope Mrs Twiddle doesn't look in the basket yet and find the clothes. What am I to *do*?'

'Twiddle, don't stand there gaping like a moon-struck goldfish!' said Mrs Twiddle, sharply. 'Go and

104

get an old suit of clothes, quickly. Do you want this poor fellow to die of cold?'

Mr Twiddle wasn't sure if he did or not, he felt in such a terrible muddle. He went upstairs to think it over, but then came down again very quickly when he remembered he had left the basket in the scullery with the fish and the suit there. He must certainly hide that basket!

He snatched up the basket, opened the scullery window and dropped the basket and its contents neatly outside under a lilac bush. There! They would be safe there till he could think what was best to do.

'Twiddle! What in the world are you doing in the scullery?'called his wife. 'You don't keep your clothes *there*! They're in the cupboard upstairs.'

Twiddle shot upstairs. He sank down on his bed. What could he do? What could he say? Nobody would believe him if he said he had thought that finding those clothes was just a bit of the good luck he had had that day. He could see himself now that it had been a very silly thing to think. But he really had thought it.

'If I go down and give him his right clothes, he might quite well haul me off to the police station and put me into prison,' thought poor Mr Twiddle. 'And if I don't give him them I shall feel really awful. He's got to have them back somehow.'

Mrs Twiddle shouted upstairs: 'TWIDDLE! *Will* you bring some clothes down at once for this poor shivering fellow? I'm just going to cook dinner quickly, so that he can have something hot. Where's the fish?'

Now Twiddle was in another muddle. The fish was in the basket underneath the lilac bush outside the scullery window. But he couldn't say that, of course. He seemed to be getting deeper and deeper into trouble. He scrabbled hastily in cupboard and took down an armful of clothes. Mrs Twiddle gave them to the wet, shivering bather, and shut him into the drawing room to change.

'Where's the fish?' she said to Twiddle, sharply.

'Er – now let me see,' said Twiddle looking very vague. 'Now – just let me see.'

A miaow suddenly came from the scullery next to the kitchen. 'There's Puss back again,' said Mrs Twiddle, and she looked pleased. 'Open the kitchen door and let her in, Twiddle. She's a real home cat – never stays away for long!'

Twiddle opened the door, feeling that his good luck had completely vanished. The cat appeared, dragging behind it a pair of fishy-smelling trousers!

Twiddle stared at the cat with great dislike. He knew at once what had happened. That tiresome animal had come home, smelt the fish in the basket lying under the clothes, and had scrabbled about in the paper and brought in the trousers, because they now smelt so deliciously of fish.

'Well! Look at that!' said Mrs Twiddle, in the greatest astonishment. 'Whatever will the cat bring in next? A pair of trousers! Where did she get them from?'

The cat disappeared, and came back again dragging a coat, which also smelt very strongly of fish. Mrs Twiddle began to think she must be in some kind of peculiar dream made up of shivering bathers, fishy clothes and a cat that came in and out with them.

Then the drawing-room door flew open and out came the bather, looking very different in Twiddle's old suit, which fitted him perfectly. He stood still and stared when he saw his coat and trousers over Mrs Twiddle's arm – and then stared even more when the cat reappeared, dragging a pair of fishy socks.

'I say – look – they're my clothes the cat is bringing in,' stammered the man, in amazement.

'*Your* clothes? Your c-c-c-. . . .' stammered Mrs Twiddle, thinking that her dream was turning into a nightmare. 'But how could Puss find them? Oh, goodness me, now she's bringing in a vest!'

The man picked up all his clothes. Mr Twiddle forced himself to speak in an ordinary kind of voice, though he was trembling inside. 'Well – if they're your clothes, perhaps you'd like to go back into the drawing room again, take off my suit, and put your own on.'

'No,' said the man, decidedly, sniffing at his clothes. 'They smell of fish. I couldn't possibly wear them till the smell is gone. If you don't mind, I'll wear yours till tomorrow, then put my own on. I'll return yours then. I'll go now – but I wish I knew where your cat got my clothes from.'

He went out of the front door and banged it shut. Mrs Twiddle stared at Mr Twiddle, feeling rather faint. She sat down in her rocking chair. 'Oh, Twiddle! I don't understand this at all. I feel quite queer. How did Puss get those clothes? Do you think she was clever enough to understand all we said, and went to hunt for them and found them?'

'No, I don't,' said Twiddle. 'It was just a bit of that cat's usual interference. She. . . .'

Mrs Twiddle alarmed him by suddenly leaping to her feet with a yell. 'Look! The cat's got the fish! Is that the fish you brought home for dinner, Twiddle? Oh, she's stolen it – she's over the wall by now. Twiddle, where did you put that fish, you silly, stupid fellow?'

'It was in the basket – er – under the lilac bush,' said poor Twiddle.

Mrs Twiddle looked at him as if he was quite mad.

'Under the *lilac* bush! But WHY? Have you gone mad, Twiddle? You'd better go to bed, I think. You must be ill.'

Twiddle thought that bed would be a very nice peaceful place, and he went up very thankfully. There was no dinner because the cat had taken the fish, but Mr Twiddle didn't mind that. It was nice to be able to pretend to be asleep, and not be asked any more awkward questions. *What* a good thing the cat had found the clothes and brought them in, after all! Now nobody would ever know the silly thing he had done in taking them home himself.

But Twiddle is going to get a shock – because that bather isn't going to come back with Twiddle's old suit! He's a dishonest fellow, and he's going to keep it. But how can Twiddle go to the police and complain about *that*? Didn't he do exactly the same thing himself, when he thought his luck was in?

Poor old Twiddle! He's not so lucky, after all!

2

Mr Twiddle's Christmas mistake

Mr Twiddle was feeling very happy. It was almost Christmas time. He had made some really beautiful Christmas cards, and had painted them himself. Most of them had robins and holly on them, because those were the two things he drew the best.

He had a cupboard full of parcels. He was going to give Mrs Twiddle a lot of nice surprises on Christmas Day. And he had bought twelve circus tickets.

Three days before Christmas the circus was coming to Twiddle's town. Twiddle loved a circus, especially one with elephants in it, and this one had three.

So he had saved up his money and had bought twelve tickets, two for himself and his wife, and ten for all their grandchildren. What a treat for them, to be sure!

'Shan't I feel grand going to the circus with ten boys and girls!' said Mr Twiddle to his wife for about the twentieth time. 'Shan't we laugh at the clowns! And clap the elephants.'

'You'll enjoy it all more than the children will, I should think,' said Mrs Twiddle; and she laughed. Sometimes she thought dear old Twiddle had never grown up.

'I'd better write the names and addresses on my Christmas cards this evening and post them,' said Mr Twiddle, four days before Christmas. 'We are asked to post early. Yes, I had better do that. Will you lend me your pen, wife?'

'Oh, dear, have you lost yours again?' said Mrs Twiddle. 'I wonder where it is this time? Yes, I'll lend you mine, Twiddle, but please don't do with it what you did last time.'

'Why, what did I do?' asked Twiddle surprised.

'You left it sticking into the vase of flowers,' said Mrs Twiddle, 'and I didn't find it till I emptied them when they were dead. I suppose you thought you had stuck it into the inkpot.'

'I'll be careful this time,' said Twiddle. He sat down at the table. He spread out all the circus tickets to look at them once more. How lovely! Twelve of them!

Then he began on his cards. He wrote the names and addresses very neatly indeed. He had done the pictures on post cards, so all he had to do was to write the address on each and stamp it.

'Now don't you be too long over those cards,' said Mrs Twiddle, looking at the clock. 'I shall want the table for supper in half an hour.'

'I'll be finished long before that,' said Twiddle, dipping his pen into his wife's little box of pins, thinking it was the ink. 'Dear me – how silly of me!'

Twiddle was longer than he had expected. He had to let the cat in when she came scratching at the door. Then he had to let the dog out. Then no sooner had he sat down again than the dog wanted to come in and the cat decided to go out.

'Those animals want a footman to wait on them,' grumbled Mr Twiddle. 'Lie down, dog!'

'He wants a drink of water,' said Mrs Twiddle. 'His bowl's empty. He's thirsty, Twiddle.'

'So am I,' said Twiddle, shaking a blot off his pen. 'My glass is empty. But I've got no one who will jump up and fill it for me unless I do it myself. So the dog can wait, too. He never does a thing for me. I'm always waiting on him.'

Well, what with one thing and another, Twiddle hadn't finished by the time Mrs Twiddle wanted the table. So he had to hurry up at the last, and he stacked all the circus tickets together and piled his Christmas cards in another heap.

'I'll go out and post the cards while you're laying the supper, wife,' he said.

'Well, take the dog for a walk,' said Mrs Twiddle. 'He'll be pleased.'

'I just wait on that dog hand and foot,' grumbled Mr Twiddle. 'And all he does is to lie about where I can keep falling over him.'

'You'd better hurry up, or you'll miss the post,' said Mrs Twiddle. 'You've only got a few minutes.'

Twiddle snatched up the pile of cards and went out. The dog went too. The cat came in as they went out and lay down by the fire. Twiddle almost fell over her.

'Why can't you look where you're going?' said Mrs Twiddle.

'Well, why doesn't the cat look where *she's* going?' asked Twiddle crossly, pulling on his coat. 'Come on, dog.'

He went into the darkness. He was soon back. The cat thought it would go out as he came in, and he nearly fell over it again. He glared at the cat's tail. 'I believe she does it on purpose,' he said.

'No,' said Mrs Twiddle. 'It's just that you are stupid, Twiddle, dear.'

'Stupid!' cried Twiddle, losing his temper. 'I like *that*! I'm the cleverest person in this house, let me tell you. Where would you all be without me? And who thought of taking all our grandchildren to the circus tomorrow, I'd like to know? Why, all you could think of for a Christmas treat for them was—'

'All right, all right, Twiddle,' said Mrs Twiddle, putting a pie down on the table with a bang. 'I agree that you're the cleverest man in the town. By the way, what did you do with my pen?'

It wasn't to be found. Oh dear, Twiddle didn't feel quite so clever, after all. He sat down to his supper gloomily. Mrs Twiddle wondered what to say to put him into a good temper again. She looked round, and saw a pile of Christmas cards on the dresser. That was why he was in such a bad temper, perhaps.

'I'm sorry you missed the post, Twiddle,' she said.

Mr Twiddle stared at her in surprise. 'I didn't miss it,' he said.

'Oh! Then why didn't you post your Christmas cards?' asked Mrs Twiddle.

'I did,' said Twiddle, thinking that his wife must be a little mad. 'I posted all of them, I heard them go into the pillar box – slip-slap.'

'How extraordinary!' said Mrs Twiddle, looking round at the Christmas cards again. 'Then why did you bring them back? How did you get them out of the postbox?'

Mr Twiddle gasped. Yes – there was no doubt about it. Mrs Twiddle must either be ill or mad. He got up and patted her on the back.

'There, there!' he said. 'Do you feel all right, love? Have you got a bad headache? There, there!'

'Don't "there, there" me like that,' said Mrs Twiddle, annoyed. 'I'm not feeling bad. All I want to know is – why did you go out to post your Christmas cards and come back with them, and yet keep on telling me you heard them go slip-slap down into the box?'

Then poor Twiddle caught sight of the pile of Christmas cards on the dresser. He stared at them. He began to wonder if he had gone mad! Hadn't he just been to post them – and hadn't he heard them go into the box – and yet here they were under his very nose! He sat down, feeling quite peculiar.

There was a little silence. Mrs Twiddle looked at Twiddle sharply. 'Twiddle,' she said, 'where are the circus tickets?'

'Er – er – I left them in a neat pile on the dresser,' said Twiddle, and he looked for them. But they weren't there.

'Well, the cat hasn't eaten them,' said Mrs Twiddle. 'What have you done with them?'

Poor Twiddle gave a sudden groan. 'Oh my, oh my! I've posted them, instead of my Christmas cards! I was in such a hurry – and what with the dog going out and the cat coming in and—'

'Don't make excuses,' said Mrs Twiddle. 'For a

man who thinks himself the cleverest in this town you're not very bright tonight, Twiddle. Now, we shan't be able to go to the circus!'

'Perhaps the postman hasn't collected the letters yet,' said Twiddle, getting up and fetching his coat. 'I'll go and see. I'll run all the way.'

The dog went with him, pleased at an extra run. He got under Twiddle's feet as usual, but Twiddle hadn't any breath to scold him. He got to the postbox – and oh, cheers, there was the postman, just emptying the box!

'I've made a mistake!' panted Twiddle. 'I've posted some tickets. Ah, yes, there they are! Could you give them me back, please?'

The postman laughed. He picked out the circus tickets and gave them to Twiddle. 'Good thing you just caught me,' he said. 'It would have been a pity to miss the circus. Good night, sir.'

Twiddle was so pleased. He rushed back home. 'I've got the tickets,' he said. 'We're all right for the circus!'

'It's a pity you forgot to take your cards to post them just now,' said Mrs Twiddle. 'Still never mind, they'll probably get there on New Year's Day. Sit down and have a cup of tea now, and finish your meal. Give me the tickets. The next thing you'll be doing is lighting the kitchen fire with them!'

Twiddle stirred his tea hard. Mrs Twiddle looked at him.

'So that's where my pen went!' she said. 'You're stirring your tea with it, Twiddle. Well, well – I'll give you a spoon to write with next time! What *is* to be done with you?'

I don't know. Do you?

3

Mr Twiddle forgets

'Twiddle, it's the New Year tomorrow,' said Mrs Twiddle, busily darning an enormous hole in one of Mr Twiddle's socks. 'New Year's Eve tonight – the time when people make good resolutions.'

'What exactly is a resolution?' asked Mr Twiddle. 'It's such a long and peculiar word.'

'Well – when you make a resolution it just means that you resolve to do something and really mean it,' said Mrs Twiddle. 'Don't pretend you don't know that, Twiddle! You make a promise to yourself – you determine to do something; but if you make this resolution on New Year's Eve it's very important and very special.'

'Oh!' said Twiddle. 'Have *you* made any good resolutions, wife?'

'Dear me, yes,' said Mrs Twiddle. 'I've resolved not to be cross with the paperboy when he brings the wrong paper – and I've resolved to mend all those old shirts of yours I've been putting off for so long – and I've resolved not to let you snore at nights—'

'Well! What a queer resolution!' said Mr Twiddle, indignantly. 'Surely that ought to be *my* resolution, not yours, wife?'

'Oh no, dear – because *you* can't stop yourself snoring, and I very well can,' said Mrs Twiddle. 'I've only got to pinch you hard and you stop.'

'Well, I don't think that's at all a nice resolution to make,' said Twiddle.

'Now, now, don't be silly. You think about your own resolutions, not mine,' said Mrs Twiddle.

Twiddle thought. 'I've got quite a lot in my mind,' he said at last. 'I'll remember to chop the wood for you. I'll remember to mend that chair leg you've been asking me about for ages. I'll resolve to be kinder to the cat – though that will be hard because she honestly does try to trip me up on purpose, I'm sure of it – still, I'll buy her some fish to show her I mean to be kind.'

'Miaow,' said the cat, thrilled, and dug its claws into Twiddle's ankles as it stretched itself.

'What do you want to do that for, you unkind, horrid creature?' shouted Twiddle, and smacked the cat.

'Well!' said Mrs Twiddle, in surprise. 'I don't

think much of your resolutions if you forget them so quickly.'

'I haven't forgotten,' said Twiddle. 'But I haven't begun them yet – it isn't New Year's Day till tomorrow. Now, let me think – I'll make a resolution to wind up the clock – and to paint the shed – and to sweep the kitchen chimney for you – and—'

'Now, Twiddle, it's not a good thing to make so *many* resolutions,' said Mrs Twiddle. 'Make ONE – one good sensible one – and keep it.'

'All right,' said Twiddle, 'I will. I know! I'll make a resolution not to forget a single thing! There – now you won't have to keep on telling me what a dreadful memory I have.'

'Splendid!' said Mrs Twiddle. 'Now you write down that resolution and put it somewhere to remind you – or else you'll forget it.'

So Twiddle wrote out his resolution in his best handwriting. 'My New Year's Resolution is that I will not forget a single thing!'

He stood it behind the clock where he could see it. He felt very pleased with himself. Aha! He would show Mrs Twiddle that he could make just as good resolutions as she could!

Next morning he heard his wife up very early. He called down in astonishment to know why she was up.

'Oh, just one of my good resolutions,' said Mrs Twiddle. 'I've determined I will never be late down in the morning. I hope you've remembered *your* resolution, Twiddle.'

Twiddle lay back in bed and thought hard. Now, what *was* his resolution? What could it have been? To be kind to the cat and get her fish? To wind up the clock? To mend something? Now WHAT was that fine, sensible resolution he had made?

He fell asleep trying to remember. It was no use, he just couldn't think of it. He was very late down for breakfast and Mrs Twiddle was cross.

'Late the first morning of the year! And what about that good resolution of yours? Have you remembered it?'

Well, Mrs Twiddle was in one of her rather bustling moods, and Twiddle simply didn't dare to tell her he had already forgotten what his good resolution was. 'You just wait and see,' he told Mrs Twiddle.

After breakfast he tried again to remember what he had resolved to do. 'Was it to chop the wood?' he wondered. 'Perhaps it was. I'll do it.'

So out he went and chopped a whole lot of wood for Mrs Twiddle. She was very pleased. But Twiddle didn't feel that had been his resolution. He tried something else. He stroked the cat and then actually went out to buy it some fish. But no – surely that wasn't his resolution? Mrs Twiddle didn't say anything to make him think it was.

Twiddle found the broken chair and mended the leg.

Now, surely *that* had been his resolution? Mrs Twiddle thanked him heartily. But she didn't say it was nice to see he had kept his resolution. So it couldn't be that.

Poor Twiddle! The things he did that day to try and find out what it was he had made a resolution about! He swept both the kitchen and the parlour chimneys and covered himself with soot. He had to have a bath, and he actually remembered to clean it after him – but somehow he didn't feel that had anything to do with his resolution either.

'I believe it was to paint the shed!' thought Mr Twiddle, and out he went to get a tin of paint and a brush.

Mrs Twiddle came out to watch. 'Well you really are good today,' she said. 'And how well you've painted the shed. Anyone would think you had made a good resolution to do it today!'

Oh dear! So he hadn't made a resolution about painting the shed. Mr Twiddle felt very gloomy. How many more things was he going to do before he remembered what his resolution really was! If only he could ask Mrs Twiddle what it was. But she would laugh at him too much. No, he really must remember it himself.

He went in to wash for tea, wondering what else there was for him to do.

Wind up the clock! Yes, of course – perhaps *that* was his good resolution. Twiddle went to the clock on the mantelpiece and hunted for the key. Mrs Twiddle looked up.

'Reading your good resolution again?' she said.

'What do you mean?' asked Twiddle – and then he suddenly saw the good resolution he had written out so neatly the night before, and stood behind the clock. There it was, staring him in the face – 'My New Year's Resolution is that I will not forget a single thing!'

So that was it – dear, dear! – and the first thing he had done was to forget what his resolution had been! Whatever would Mrs Twiddle say if she knew?

'You've remembered your resolution marvellously, I think,' she said. 'Really marvellously! You haven't forgotten a single thing all day long, Twiddle. I do feel pleased. I shall cook you a very special kipper for your tea!'

He did enjoy his kipper – but, you know, he didn't say a word to Mrs Twiddle about forgetting his resolution – not one single word. It's still there, behind the clock. I wonder how soon he'll forget it again!

4

Twiddle in trouble again

Mr Twiddle was sitting by the fire reading his paper. The windows were shut. It was nice and warm and cosy.

Then the cat pushed at the door, opened it wide, and strolled into the room. A cold draught at once blew down Mr Twiddle's neck.

He looked round, and then spoke crossly to Mrs Twiddle, who was sitting on the opposite side of the fireplace.

'Wife, I wish you'd teach your cat to shut the door after her. She comes in and leaves it wide open – and *I* have to get up and shut it.'

'You can't teach cats things like that,' said Mrs Twiddle, sleepily.

'You can teach dogs all kinds of tricks,' grumbled Mr Twiddle. 'Shut the door, Puss!'

The cat sat down and washed itself. It always did that when it saw that Twiddle was cross. It knew it annoyed him.

'Oh, do get up and shut the door, Twiddle,' said his wife. 'There's such a draught.'

Twiddle got up, grumbling. He shut the door and came back to his chair. The cat was now lying on it, fast asleep.

'Look at that!' said Twiddle. 'It not only leaves the door open for me to shut, but takes my chair, too, and then pretends to be asleep.'

He turned the cat off his chair. It at once went to a window, and mewed. 'Let it out, Twiddle, dear,' said Mrs Twiddle.

'But it's only just come in,' said Twiddle, exasperated.

'Well, it wants to go out again,' said Mrs Twiddle.

So Twiddle got up, opened the window and let the cat out. He banged the window shut so hard that the cat leapt into the air with fright. So did Mrs Twiddle.

'Twiddle! Don't do things like that!' she said. 'I've told you before, and. . . .'

Twiddle sat down and closed his eyes. He thought if he pretended to be asleep, Mrs Twiddle wouldn't go on scolding him. But she did. However, in a few minutes Twiddle really was asleep.

He was awakened by a very cold draught blowing round his neck. He sat up and looked round. The door was wide open again.

'The cat's just come in,' said Mrs Twiddle. 'I expect she found it cold outside today, poor lamb. Would you shut the door, Twiddle?'

Then Twiddle lost his temper. He swooped on the astonished cat, caught tight hold of it, and ran upstairs with it. He pushed it into the spare bedroom, where all the windows were tightly closed and then slammed and locked the door.

'Now, you just stay there, where you can't get out *or* in!' said Twiddle. 'Making me open windows and shut doors all the afternoon! Grrrrrrrr!'

The cat settled down in the middle of the eiderdown, purring. Twiddle went downstairs, looking fierce. 'Now, wife, listen to me – that cat stays there all the afternoon, do you hear?'

Mrs Twiddle knew she couldn't do anything with Twiddle when he really was in a temper, so she didn't say anything at all.

Presently there was a peculiar noise from upstairs.
The boards creaked loudly, as if someone was walking over the spare-room floor.

'Whatever's that?' said Mrs Twiddle, looking
alarmed, and she half-rose to go up to see.

'Sit down,' said Twiddle. 'You know it's the cat.
I'm not going to let you go upstairs and let her out.
Sit down. She's just walking about.'

'But you can't usually hear cats walk!' cried Mrs
Twiddle.

'She's probably stamping around in a temper,'
said Twiddle. 'Sit down!'

Soon there was another noise, as if something was
falling. Mrs Twiddle leapt up. 'I must go and see
what's happening!'

'SIT DOWN!' roared Twiddle. 'It's the cat
walking about on the dressing table, that's all, and
knocking over the candlesticks!'

'But the cat never walks on the dressing table,' said Mrs Twiddle. Still, she sat down, because Twiddle really did look so very fierce.

Presently there was a squeaking noise, and Mrs Twiddle looked up to the ceiling, above which was the spare room. 'What's that?' she said.

'The cat squealing,' said Twiddle, pleased. 'Let it squeal. Do it good. It's got nobody to open and shut doors and windows for it up there and it's angry.'

'But that squeak sounded exactly as if the wardrobe door was being opened,' said Mrs Twiddle, alarmed. 'It always squeaks like that.'

'Well, I daresay your cat can open wardrobe doors as easily as it can open the kitchen door, and make a draught down my neck,' said Twiddle. 'Sit down, wife!'

After that there was a curious slithering sound, and then nothing at all. Mrs Twiddle went on with her knitting. Twiddle fell asleep. But he was awakened once more by a draught blowing down his neck, and when he turned round, there was the door opening wide again – and the cat walking in, purring loudly!

'Puss dear! Clever Puss! How did you get out of the spare room?' said Mrs Twiddle, pleased. 'Twiddle, isn't she clever! How in the world did she manage it?'

Twiddle stared at the cat, astonished and angry. It *couldn't* get out of the spare room – and yet there it was!

'It must be another cat!' said Twiddle at last. 'Our own *must* be in the spare room. Why, I *locked* it in!'

Twiddle went up to the spare room. How queer – the door was still locked! And the windows had been closed – so how *could* the cat have got out? He unlocked the door and looked in.

The window was wide open! The wardrobe door was wide open, too – and Twiddle's best coat was gone! The drawers of the chest were open, and Mrs Twiddle's best bed cover, which was kept there, was gone. So were the silver candlesticks off the dressing table, and the clock from the mantelpiece. Oh dear, what could have happened?

Mrs Twiddle heard Twiddle's groan and came hurrying up. When she saw what had happened, she burst into tears.

'A burglar came! He must have climbed up the gutter pipe whilst we were in the kitchen, and he tramped about overhead and opened drawers, and knocked things over, and opened the wardrobe door

which squeaks – and we heard everything – and you said it was the cat! If you hadn't been unkind to the cat, and shut her in here, and said *she* made all the noise, poor lamb, we'd have shot up to the spare room and caught the burglar at once!'

Twiddle felt very, very uncomfortable. He had to tell the whole story to the police later on, and they tried hard not to laugh.

'I hope you'll never be hard on poor Puss again,' said Mrs Twiddle that evening.

'I wasn't hard on her,' said Twiddle. '*She's* hard on *me* – making me shut doors and—'

'Now, that's enough!' said Mrs Twiddle. 'You've done enough damage for *one* day, Twiddle, losing your temper. Don't lose it again. Look, take the cat for me a minute. I've got to peep in the oven.'

And will you believe it, poor Twiddle had to nurse the cat the whole evening. She purred so loudly that he couldn't hear the wireless properly. What a shame!

5

Twiddle cuts the grass

'I do wish,' said Mrs Twiddle, 'I *do* wish, Twiddle, that you would do something about that long grass in the garden. It looks so very untidy.'

Mrs Twiddle said this almost every day. Mr Twiddle sighed. He knew he would have to cut that grass sooner or later. Well, it was a nice day. He might as well do it and get it over.

'Very well, my love,' he said. 'I'll take the scythe and mow it down. Anything to please you!'

'Well, put your garden trousers on, dear,' said Mrs Twiddle. 'You don't want to spoil your nice ones.'

Twiddle went upstairs and found his garden trousers. They were old grey flannel ones and he liked them. They were big and comfortable.

He put them on and then took everything out of the pockets of his other trousers and put them into the pockets of his garden trousers. In went his money, his keys, his handkerchief and a little roll of string that he always kept in case he might want some.

Then he went downstairs to find the scythe. 'It may be blunt, of course,' he said to Mrs Twiddle. 'Then I couldn't start mowing the grass today.'

'Well, it isn't blunt,' said Mrs Twiddle. 'I had it sharpened last week for you. Now do get to work, Twiddle – you've been ages already getting your garden trousers on.'

Twiddle went out into the garden. It was rather hot. Oh dear, scything was very very hard work! He would soon be dreadfully hot! He took off his coat.

He walked to the long grass with the big scythe in his hand. Dear, dear, it certainly was very long! He felt the blade of the scythe to see if it really was sharp, and it was.

Now, just as Mr Twiddle was about to begin his work, the cat walked over to him, and rubbed against his leg in a very loving manner. Twiddle was not very fond of his wife's cat. It always wanted doors or windows opened for it whenever Twiddle was sitting down reading his paper.

'Go away, Puss!' he said, sternly. 'I'm going to do a bit of scything. You don't want your tail cut off, do you? Well, use your brains then, and get away. Shoo!'

The cat rubbed itself against Mr Twiddle's other leg. Then it sat down and began to wash itself.

'Did you hear what I said?' asked Twiddle. 'Go away from this long grass. Right away. Surely you would not be silly enough to lie down and sleep in it just when I'm going to scythe it? Of course, I know that's just the kind of thing you *would* do!'

The cat immediately curled itself up in the grass and tucked its head into its paws. Twiddle stirred it with his foot.

'Now, what did I say? Go and find Mrs Twiddle! Go along!'

The cat uncurled itself, went a little way away, gave Twiddle a nasty look and settled down again. Mr Twiddle began to get angry. He ran at the cat.

'Shoo! Get away! Why do you always make things difficult for me?'

The cat decided that Twiddle wanted to have a game with it. It jumped up, crouched down, and ran at Twiddle's feet. Then it darted away into the grass and hid. Twiddle ran at it again. 'Shoo! *Will* you go away and let me get on with my work?'

Mrs Twiddle put her head out of the window. 'Twiddle! What *are* you doing rushing about in the grass all by yourself and shouting like that?'

'I'm *not* all by myself!' shouted back Twiddle, indignantly. 'The cat's here. How can I cut the grass if she's darting about the whole time?'

He chased the cat all about the grass and at last it ran off to Mrs Twiddle, its tail straight up in the air. Twiddle, feeling very hot, panted a bit, and then lifted the scythe.

But just as he was about to begin his work he saw something lying in the grass, something bright and round. He picked it up. A sixpence! Well, that was a nice little find. Very nice, indeed. He put it into his pocket with his other money.

'It's a pity I can't find a bit more money,' he said to himself. 'If I could I'd pay a man to do this heavy scything.'

He cut a piece of grass – and then he suddenly saw something shining once more. He bent down – goodness gracious, it was a shilling!

'Very strange!' said Mr Twiddle. 'Someone's been walking in this grass, I suppose, and dropped a bit of money. Who's been trespassing in my garden? Well, it serves him right to lose his money!'

He lifted his scythe again, and then thought that he might as well have a look to see if there was any more money lying in the long grass. So he put down his scythe and began to look.

He soon saw a penny and a ha'penny! Then he found another sixpence. Well, well, this *was* a nice surprise, to be sure! 'Two shillings and a penny ha'penny altogether. Splendid!'

He began to look very carefully indeed, bending down and peering in the grass, parting the long blades hopefully.

'Another shilling! Well, I never! And here's half a crown. Would you believe it! Why, this bit of grass is full of money!'

It was most extraordinary. He kept on picking up pennies and ha'pennies, sixpences and shillings wherever he looked. He put them all into his pocket, feeling very pleased indeed. 'I shall get a man to come and do the scything now. Why, I must have picked up about a pound's worth of money already. Very nice, very nice indeed!'

Mrs Twiddle looked out of the window again to see if Twiddle was getting on well with his scything. She saw him bending down, creeping here and there, then suddenly standing up to put something into his pocket, then bending down again and creeping about. What *was* he doing?

'Twiddle!' shouted Mrs Twiddle. 'What *do* you

think you're doing? Surely you're not playing with the cat?'

'I am *not*!' said Twiddle, standing up, looking rather hot. 'I'm picking up money.'

'Good gracious!' said Mrs Twiddle. 'Money! Whatever do you mean?'

'What I say,' said Twiddle, and bent down to pick up a sixpence. He held it up to show her. 'It's easy. I just look for it and I see it. It's all over this piece of grass. Wherever I go I find pennies and ha'pennies and sixpences and shillings and half-crowns. Why here's half a crown by my foot now!'

So there was. Mrs Twiddle hurried down to the patch of long grass. 'Really, Twiddle! I can't believe it. How could there be so much money in this grass? Where in the world did it come from?'

'Somebody must have dropped it,' said Twiddle. 'Somebody trespassing in my garden. Serves him right to lose it.'

He picked up a sixpence and put it into his pocket. 'I'm going to pay a man to do this scything instead of me,' he said. 'And if you'd like to buy yourself a box of chocolates, wife, I'd be pleased to give you the money. And we might perhaps buy a chicken for our dinner.'

Mrs Twiddle looked very puzzled. She couldn't understand this money business at all. Twiddle wandered away a little and then picked up a penny. 'See! I tell you wherever I go in this grass I pick up money.'

'Your pocket must be absolutely full of it!' said Mrs Twiddle. 'How much have you got?'

'Well, I've picked up dozens and dozens of pennies and sixpences and shillings and things,' said Twiddle. 'I'll show you what I've got.'

He put his hand into his pocket to get out all the

money he had put there. He felt round his pocket and a frown came on his face.

'What's the matter?' said Mrs Twiddle.

'Most extraordinary thing,' said Twiddle, looking astonished, 'I can't feel even a *penny* in my pocket! And yet I put dozens of coins there. Where have they all gone?'

'Let *me* feel,' said Mrs Twiddle, and she put her hand into his pocket. She felt around – and then she found a big hole at the bottom!

'Twiddle! You've got an enormous hole in that pocket. I really do think you are the very stupidest man I've ever known! Here you go walking about with a hole in your pocket, dropping all your money out, and picking it up and putting it in your pocket again and then out it falls, and you pick it up all over again – and think you're so rich we can have chicken for dinner!'

Mr Twiddle stared at his wife in dismay. He felt the hole in his pocket. 'Have I – have I been picking up the same penny and the same sixpence, and the same shilling all the time?' he said. 'Wasn't this grass full of money, then?'

'No, you stupid man! Whatever money was here fell from your pocket – when you were chasing the cat about, I should think,' said Mrs Twiddle. 'And you kept on picking it up and losing it and picking it up . . . oh, Twiddle, I think my cat's got more sense in its head than you have. Wasting all the morning doing a silly thing like that!'

Twiddle was very upset. He picked up a shilling by his foot and absent-mindedly put it into his pocket. It at once fell out and appeared by his foot again.

'See! That's what's been happening all the time,' said Mrs Twiddle. 'Now, you listen to me, Twiddle – I shan't give you any dinner at all till you've finished

cutting this grass. So, if you want to play with the cat or go on picking up your money, you know what to expect!'

And little Mrs Twiddle walked back to the house quite crossly. Twiddle sighed loudly, took his scythe and set to work.

What a disappointment – and how cross Mrs Twiddle looked. Then a thought came into Twiddle's head. He threw down his scythe and ran across the garden till he came to the kitchen window. He popped his head in and made Mrs Twiddle jump.

'Now, you listen to me,' said Twiddle, quite fiercely. 'Do you know whose fault all this is? Yours, wife, yours! And do you know why? Because you didn't mend the hole in my pocket! Aha! Aha!'

Then, feeling quite pleased with himself, Twiddle went happily back to the grass and scythed hard till it was all cut. And you will be glad to know that Mrs Twiddle had a lovely dinner ready for him, and gave him a hearty kiss when he came in.

'You're a dear old thing, even if you *are* a stupid!' she said. 'Now, don't you dare to say Aha! to me again, or I shall laugh till I cry. Aha, indeed!'

6

A knot in Twiddle's hanky

'I do wish I could remember things,' said Mr Twiddle in despair. 'I meant to go and fetch my shoes before the shops closed, so that I could go for a nice walk this evening – and I forgot.'

'And you can't possibly go for a walk in those old shoes you're wearing,' said Mrs Twiddle. 'Why don't you tie a knot in your hanky, or something, Twiddle, then you would see it and remember you had to do something?'

'Well, that's just what I *will* do!' said Mr Twiddle, and he took out his big red handkerchief and tied a large knot at one corner. 'There! Now, when I see that knot I shall know I must remember something.'

'What are you going to remember?' asked Mrs Twiddle, with a little squeal of laughter.

'Oh, dear me, yes – I forgot I had to have something to remember, before I tied a knot,' said Mr Twiddle. 'Well, I know – I really must remember to fetch my shoes tomorrow. I'll leave the knot in for that.'

So he left it in, and went to read his paper in the garden. Before very long he took out his red hanky to mop his head – and he saw the knot.

'Aha! The knot! Now that was to make sure I remembered something. What was it?

But for the life of him poor Mr Twiddle couldn't remember what the knot was for! So he called his wife. 'Wife, can you think of anything I said I would do, and haven't done?' he asked.

'Good gracious, yes!' said Mrs Twiddle at once, thinking of a whole lot of things. 'What about cutting the grass?'

'Oh, dear – did I really put the knot in my hanky for that?' said Mr Twiddle, with a sigh. 'Well, well – it's no good putting knots in if I don't take any notice of them.' So he got up, fetched the mowing machine and began to cut the grass.

He was so hot when he had finished that he sat down on the seat to rest. He pulled out his hanky – and in it he saw the knot again. He had forgotten to undo it! So he thought it was another knot, of course. He stared at it, frowning.

'Good gracious! Now what's *this* knot for?' he wondered. He called to his wife. 'Is there anything else I ought to do?'

'Dear me, yes! What about weeding the lettuces?' called back his wife, giggling to herself to think that dear old Twiddle hadn't undone the knot.

Twiddle got up. 'Well, I never! Was that what the knot was for in my hanky? What a memory I've got, to be sure.'

So off he went to weed the lettuce bed, and it took him till supper time. He was really very tired when he went in.

After his supper he took out his hanky to wipe some crumbs off his waistcoat – and again he saw the very same knot.

'Look at that!' he said to his wife, who turned away to laugh all by herself. 'What's *that* knot for, I'd like to know?'

'You haven't filled the coke bucket for me,' said Mrs Twiddle. 'Would it be that, Twiddle?'

'It might be,' said Twiddle. 'Anyway, I'll do it. Oh dear, what a pity I saw the knot!'

He saw it again just before he went to bed. 'Bless us all! Here's a knot in my hanky again!' he said to his wife. 'The things I have to remember! What can it be now? Is there anything important I must do?'

'Yes. Put the cat out, and then get her in again,' said Mrs Twiddle, lighting her candle to go up to bed. 'You always forget that, Twiddle.'

Twiddle groaned. 'That cat! I let her in and out all day long. She just does it on purpose. And yet at night, when I kindly open the door for her without her asking me, she won't go out. Puss, come along! Out you go!'

Mrs Twiddle had gone upstairs by the time Mr Twiddle had let the cat out and waited patiently for it to come back again. He went up with his candle and got into bed beside his plump little wife.

He took his hanky to put under the pillow – and dear me, he saw the knot again! Yes, the very same knot!

Mrs Twiddle was asleep. Twiddle couldn't bear to waken her. He stared at the knot and tried to puzzle out what it was there to remind him of. To fasten all the windows? To rake out the kitchen fire? To see if the larder door was safely shut? To – to – to – well, what *was* the knot for?

Poor Twiddle got out of bed, put on his dressing gown and went downstairs to see if he could find something he had forgotten to do. But he couldn't. The doors were locked, the windows were fastened, the larder was shut, the fire was raked out. Then what could it be?

He went into the sitting room to see if everything was all right there, and fell over the cat, which got between his legs in her usual annoying way. He fell down with a crash, knocked over a little table, and down went Mrs Twiddle's pet fern!

Mrs Twiddle woke up with a dreadful jump. 'Twiddle!' she said sharply. 'Burglars! Quick, Twiddle!'

But Twiddle wasn't there. Mrs Twiddle put on her dressing gown and went downstairs in time to see Twiddle pelting the cat with the earth out of her plant pot! She was very cross indeed.

'Really, Twiddle! Have you *got* to do this sort of thing in the middle of the night when I'm sound asleep? The poor cat! And my poor fern! Puss, Puss, come to me, then. Naughty Twiddle, what was he doing to you?

'*Well*!' said Twiddle, annoyed. 'I like *that*! Why don't you ask your cat what she was doing to *me*? Tripping me up on purpose!'

'What did you come down for?' asked Mrs Twiddle, crossly.

'Well – to see if I'd forgotten to do something,' said Twiddle. 'But everything seems all right. I'm coming to bed. But that cat isn't, wife. Leave her in the kitchen, please.'

'Poor Pussy!' said Mrs Twiddle, and put the cat down. They went up to bed together and took off their dressing gowns. Just as he got into bed Twiddle saw his hanky on the pillow and stared at the knot.

'That knot again!' he cried. 'What's it to remind me of *now*, I'd like to know. I'll never put another knot in my hanky again!'

'You won't need to!' said Mrs Twiddle, with a laugh. 'You seem to keep the same one in all the time. You never undo it! Oh, Twiddle, you'll be the death of me one day, with your foolish ways. Now, you listen to me – that knot is to tell you to lie down, shut your eyes and go to sleep!'

'Is it really?' said Twiddle, blowing out his candle and lying down very thankfully. 'Well, well, well – to

140

think I put a knot in my hanky to remind me to do something I could *never* forget to do!'

And off he went to sleep. But I wonder if he'll remember to fetch his shoes next day? Do you think he will?

7

Mr Twiddle goes shopping

'Twiddle, you are not listening to anything I'm saying!' said Mrs Twiddle, crossly. 'There you sit in your chair, reading your newspaper and not paying any attention to me at all.'

'But you were only talking about your shopping, my love,' said Mr Twiddle.

'I know – but *you* are to do the shopping for me today, so I want you to listen!' scolded Mrs Twiddle.

'Aren't you going to make me out a list?' said Mr Twiddle. 'You always take a list yourself.'

'Yes, of course I shall make you a list – but you must listen to me all the same,' said Mrs Twiddle.

'Very well, my dear,' said Mr Twiddle, but he didn't listen. He went on reading his paper, and all that Mrs Twiddle said went in at one ear and out at the other.

Somebody came to the door and Mrs Twiddle went to open it. When she came back, she had Twiddle's hat and coat and scarf in her hands.

'Here you are, Twiddle,' she said. 'Put these on and go quickly, or everything in the shops will be sold. Hurry!'

'You always want things done in such a hurry,' grumbled Twiddle, putting down his paper and getting up.

He put on his coat and hat and Mrs Twiddle tied his scarf round his neck. Then she gave him a kiss. 'There you are, grumbler. And here is your shopping list.

Take the basket and be sure to bring me back everything on the list.'

Twiddle put the list in his pocket, picked up the basket, fell over the cat, and went out. It was a nice, bright, frosty day. Twiddle walked fast because it was cold.

He looked at his list. 'Butter, Soles, Drops, Corn, Hooks, Cake,' he read. 'Well, butter is easy. I'll call at the grocer's for that straight away.'

He collected the butter. 'Soles,' he thought. 'Good gracious! Does Mrs Twiddle want soles for her shoes – or soles to eat? Goodness knows!'

He thought the best thing to do would be to buy a pair of soles at the fish shop, and a pair of soles at the shoe shop. Then whatever happened, he would be right. So that is what he did! Into his basket went the fish, also the soles to go inside slippers.

He looked at the list again. 'Drops! Goodness gracious, what kind of drops? Snowdrops? Peppermint drops? Eye drops? Which did Mrs Twiddle say?'

Well, of course, as Twiddle hadn't listened at all to what Mrs Twiddle said to him he had no idea which to buy. He decided to get some more eye drops at the chemist's. Mrs Twiddle had weak eyes and she sometimes put drops into them at night. She might have meant those.

On the other hand she might have meant peppermint drops, which she liked very much. Very well, Mr Twiddle would get those too! So he went to the sweet shop and bought sixpenny-worth of peppermint drops.

Then he suddenly saw a woman selling bunches of snowdrops at the kerb. Snow*drops*! Well, well – Mrs Twiddle *might* have meant those. So he bought a little bunch and put it into his basket.

What was next on the list? Corn? Ah, corn, that was easy. But wait a minute – did Mrs Twiddle want corn for her hens, or a corn cure for that big corn she was always complaining about? Twiddle decided to buy both, then Mrs Twiddle couldn't possibly grumble at him.

So he bought a bag of corn, which was very heavy, and a bottle of corn cure. What next?

'Hooks. Hooks! Gracious, what kind of hooks? Hooks and eyes – curtain hooks – or crochet hooks?' wondered poor Mr Twiddle. 'Can't be curtain hooks, because she isn't hanging up any curtains. It must be crochet hooks – or hooks and eyes, I'll buy both and after that I'll buy the cake.'

It was a very, very heavy basket that Mr Twiddle took home. He decided to ask Mrs Twiddle to read down the list to him, and then he would hand out the things she said – perhaps she would add a little explanation as she read them. She might say 'soles for our supper,' then he would know that meant the fish, and not the slipper soles, and he could hand out the right thing.

'Hallo, Twiddle dear, what a long time you've been!' said Mrs Twiddle, when he went into the house. 'Have you got everything? I do hope you have. They were all most important.'

Mr Twiddle hoped he had got them too. Mrs Twiddle wouldn't be at all pleased if he had brought the wrong things!

'Read down the list, dear, and I'll hand out the things,' said Twiddle. Mrs Twiddle took the list and began to read. 'Butter, Twiddle – did you get it?'

'Here it is,' said Twiddle, and handed it out. 'Next, please?'

'Soles, Twiddle. I do hope the fishmonger hadn't

144

sold out,' said Mrs Twiddle. That was a most helpful remark. Mr Twiddle at once handed out the fish.

'The drops,' said Mrs Twiddle. 'Had the chemist got them?'

'Ah,' thought Twiddle, as he handed out the eye drops, 'this is fine! What a good idea of mine to get Mrs Twiddle to read out the list!'

'Corn,' said Mrs Twiddle. 'Ah, there it is in that bag. What a lovely lot you've brought, Twiddle! The hens *will* enjoy themselves!'

'Easier and easier!' thought Twiddle, feeling very pleased. 'What's next, wife?'

'Hooks,' said Mrs Twiddle. 'Did you get them?'

Ah – now Twiddle didn't know which hooks to hand out – the hooks and eyes – or the crochet hooks! He pretended to stop and think whether he had got them or not.

'Oh, don't say you forgot my hooks and eyes!' said

Mrs Twiddle. 'I *told* you I wanted to sew them on to my new dress tonight. Oh, Twiddle!'

'Yes, yes, I got them!' said Twiddle delighted, and handed out the little packet. 'And here's the cake. That was the last thing on the list, wasn't it?'

'How clever you are!' said Mrs Twiddle. She looked at the basket. 'Why, you've got lots more things there, Twiddle? Snowdrops! How lovely! Are they for me?'

'Yes,' said Twiddle, beaming. 'Of course.'

'Oh, how kind you are. And what are these?' said Mrs Twiddle, opening a bag. '*Pepper*mint drops! How did you guess I had none left? And, oh, Twiddle, you don't mean to tell me you remembered to buy a pair of soles to put in my old bedroom slippers! How wonderful!'

'Well,' began Twiddle, 'you see. . . .'

But Mrs Twiddle cut him short and gave him a hug. 'Thank you, thank you,' she said. 'They're lovely and just the right size.'

She dived into the basket again. 'Oh, Twiddle, you've bought me a new corn cure for my poor corn – and you've got some new crochet hooks for me, too. You are really very kind and generous!'

Twiddle felt so pleased. He had done better than he thought! Mrs Twiddle flew round him; and found his slippers and his pipe. She gave him his newspaper, and made up the fire.

'Now you sit down and have a good read!' she said. 'And I'll make you toast and dripping for your tea. You deserve a treat, you nice, kind man!'

Well, he did really, didn't he – and how he enjoyed it!

8

Mr Twiddle and the shears

'Twiddle!' called Mrs Twiddle. 'Are you going down into the town today?'

Twiddle put down his newspaper and groaned. He knew what that question meant. It meant that Mrs Twiddle had a whole lot of shopping for him to do. But for once in a way he was mistaken. She didn't want any shopping done, she only wanted something taken to be sharpened.

'It's the garden shears,' she said. 'They are so very blunt that I can't cut the edges of the grass with them. Could you take them to be mended?'

Well, as the shop that mended such things as shears stood just beside the river, where Mr Twiddle loved to watch the passing ships, he was quite pleased to go. 'Yes, I'll go down into the town, now,' he said. 'If I go now I can watch the twelve o'clock steamer passing under the bridge.'

He was very pleased about that. He liked watching the steamer, especially when it was crammed full of people. They all waved to him and that made Twiddle feel very important.

He folded up his paper, put it in his chair ready for when he came home, and went to get his hat and stick. He set off happily.

It was almost twelve o'clock when he got to the bridge. There came the steamer, flags flying, and a band playing – lovely!

Everyone waved to Mr Twiddle and he waved back happily with his hat. Really, he might be a king, the way he felt when he saw hundreds of people waving like that!

The steamer passed by. Mr Twiddle put on his hat again and went into the ironmonger's shop. 'Yes, sir? What can I do for you?' asked the boy behind the counter.

'I want some garden shears mended,' said Mr Twiddle.

'Shall we fetch them, sir?' asked the boy.

'No, I've. . . .' began Mr Twiddle, and then he stopped. Dear me – where were the shears? He hadn't got them with him! What had he done with them?

'Er – I must have left them somewhere,' said Twiddle, and hurried out of the shop. Yes – he had left them at home! He rushed back, and Mrs Twiddle met him at the door.

'You're in nice time for your dinner, Twiddle,' she said, pleased. 'When did they say they would have the shears mended? Today?'

'Well, er – you see – the fact is, I didn't take them,' said Twiddle, going rather red. 'I quite forgot them, wife. There they are, on the hall table.'

'Really, Twiddle! You do some silly things, I know – but fancy going off to ask for shears to be mended, and leaving them behind all the time!' said Mrs Twiddle, vexed. 'It's too bad of you.'

'Yes, it is,' said Twiddle. 'I'll take them this afternoon.'

So, after he had had his dinner, he got his hat and his stick. 'Mind you take the shears, too!' said Mrs Twiddle, calling from the kitchen.

'I've got them under my arm,' said Twiddle. 'Don't worry!'

Off he went with the shears. It was a lovely day and soon he overtook his old friend Mr Wander. Mr Wander was a great walker, and knew all the little highways and byways of the countryside.

'Where are you going?' he asked Twiddle.

'Nowhere particular,' said Twiddle. 'Just taking these shears along, that's all. I'll come with you a little way, it's such a nice afternoon.'

Well, Twiddle and Wander talked and walked and really enjoyed each other's company. When at last Twiddle found himself back at his front gate, he beamed at Wander and shook him warmly by the hand. 'It's a long time since I enjoyed a walk and a talk so much!' he said, and indoors he went.

Mrs Twiddle came to meet him. 'Oh, Twiddle – how lovely! You've waited for the shears to be sharpened and brought them home for me. That *is* nice of you!'

Twiddle stared down at the shears in horror.

149

Gracious! He had carried them all the way there and back and hadn't even gone into the shop! They were as blunt as when he had set off with them.

It was very, very difficult to explain this to Mrs Twiddle. She kept saying, 'But how *could* you carry the shears under your arm all that way and never once think of getting them sharpened?' Mr Twiddle felt very foolish and could hardly eat any tea at all.

'Now, tomorrow morning you're to go straight to the shop with those shears, and you're to wait there till they're done,' said Mrs Twiddle. 'First you go without them, then you take them all the way there and back and don't have them sharpened – now you just see that you wait for them!'

So the next morning poor Twiddle had no time to read his paper. He had to set off at once with the shears. Oh dear – suppose the shop couldn't do them till the afternoon? What about his dinner? He would have to go without it if he waited for the shears!

He arrived safely at the shop and was glad to see that the shears were still under his arm. Good! Now to ask the boy when they could be done.

'Yes? Brought the shears this time, I see,' said the boy with a grin. 'You want them sharpened, I suppose, sir?'

'Yes, please,' said Twiddle. 'When can you do them? I'm – er – well, I'm in a bit of a hurry.'

'Can't do them before two o'clock, sir,' said the boy, looking at a list of work to be done. 'Very sorry.'

Mr Twiddle groaned. He would certainly not get home for dinner, then, because he had promised his wife to wait for the shears. 'All right,' he said. 'I'll wait for them.'

He sat down in the shop, and wished he hadn't left his newspaper at home. Then, after a while, he remembered that the eleven o'clock steamer would soon be along. He cheered up a bit. He could go and watch that, and the twelve o'clock one, too – *and* the one o'clock – yes, and he could see the two o'clock one go by as well, just before he collected the shears. Well, well, it wasn't often that he had the chance of watching four steamers in one day.

He went off to wait for the eleven o'clock steamer. He sat in the sun and snoozed, and most unfortunately missed the steamer when it went by. Never mind, he could see the twelve o'clock.

He did, and everyone waved like mad again. Mr Twiddle waved back so madly that he almost dropped his hat in the water.

At half-past twelve he began to feel very hungry. He considered what to do. He couldn't go home to his dinner because Mrs Twiddle would be very angry to see him coming home again without the shears. But, if he had enough money in his pocket, he could go and have a nice dinner in the little inn nearby, the one that faced on to the river.

'Then I can watch the boats go by all the time,' he thought happily. 'Really, this day is turning out to be quite a nice one for me, after all.'

He went to the shop to find out how much the shears would be when they were sharpened. Then he would know how much money he would be able to spend on his dinner. The boy was still there, behind the counter.

'Your shears aren't ready yet, sir,' he said. 'I said two o'clock, you know.'

'Yes, I know,' said Mr Twiddle. 'I just came in to find out how much they will be when they are done.'

'Two shillings and sixpence, sir,' said the boy.

'Thank you,' said Twiddle. 'I'll be in at two o'clock to fetch them. I may as well pay for them

151

now, then I can just take the shears and go, when I come in after dinner.'

He paid the two shillings and sixpence and went out. Now he could spend the rest of his money on his dinner. He had four shillings and sixpence. He could get a nice meal at the inn for that.

He watched the one o'clock steamer go by and then went to get his dinner. It was lovely to sit in the window of the inn, eating cold meat and salad, and be able to watch the ships and barges go by at the same time.

He waited for the two o'clock steamer to pass, and then he paid his bill, and walked back to the iron-monger's shop. He went in.

There was nobody there! The boy was lazy and never came back from his dinner at the right time. Bother him!

Twiddle saw a long parcel lying at one end of the counter. It had a ticket on it. Twiddle looked at it,

feeling sure that it was his shears. The ticket said 2s. 6d.

'Half a crown – yes, this is my parcel,' he said, pleased. 'Well, as I've paid the bill I don't see why I can't collect these shears and go. It's not my fault that the boy is so late back from his dinner.'

So he put the parcel under his arm and off he went. Mrs Twiddle was out in the garden, trying to cut the grass edges with an old pair of shears. She was very pleased to see him.

'Ah, good!' she said. 'You've brought them back at last – sharpened this time, I hope! How much were they?'

'Two and six,' said Twiddle, and Mrs Twiddle tut-tutted and said that was a dreadful price. She tore the paper off – and then gave a scream.

'Twiddle! What's this? It's a saw! A *saw*! Do you mean to tell me you took our saw to be sharpened instead of the shears? Well, really, REALLY! I don't know what to say to you, honestly I don't.'

All the same, she said a lot, and Twiddle had to listen. He was puzzled. *Had* he taken the saw instead of the shears? No – he knew he hadn't. Then he had taken somebody else's parcel instead of his own. What a tiresome nuisance.

'Oh – so that's the next silly thing you did is it?' said Mrs Twiddle. 'Well, I'll give you one more chance of being silly – you can just take this saw back to the shop straight away and get the shears instead!'

So off went poor Mr Twiddle once more. He came to the shop and told the boy what had happened.

'I've brought back the saw, so can I take my shears now?' he asked.

'Oh my!' said the boy. 'I must have given them to the other customer, when he came for his saw. They were wrapped up, too, you see. He lives at Romer Green, five miles away.'

Well, well, well! – that was too much for Mr Twiddle altogether. He looked desperately round the shop. He saw a pair of brand-new shears hanging there.

'I'll buy these,' he said. 'Give them to me now. I'll come in and pay for them tomorrow.'

And he went off home with a new pair of shears for Mrs Twiddle – but whether she'll be pleased or not about that I really don't know. Twiddle does really do some peculiar things, doesn't he?

9

Mr Twiddle's shadow

Mr Twiddle was very angry with the cat. He spoke to it very sternly indeed.

'Now you listen to me, Cat! You have a good home here and plenty to eat, and a nice basket of your own. And what do you do? You steal things out of the larder if the door is left open so much as a crack, and you. . . .'

The cat turned its back on Mr Twiddle and began to wash itself, wetting its paws and rubbing them over its face.

'Turn round!' said Mr Twiddle, in a rage. 'Don't you know your manners? I'm talking to you. Stop doing that soap-and-flannel act of yours, washing your silly face over and over, and look at me!'

The cat didn't. It just went on washing itself. Twiddle marched round to the other side of it and addressed it again.

'All right! If you think you can turn your back on me, you're wrong. Now, just let me tell you the things you've done to annoy me today. I left the breakfast table for just one moment and what did you do? Jumped up and ate all my bacon. And you. . . .'

The cat turned its back to Twiddle again and began to wash another bit of itself. Twiddle flew into a real temper and stamped his foot. He began to shout.

'Rude creature! You stole my bacon, you made me open the window twice – once for you to come in and once for you to go out – and you tripped me up in the passage when I was carrying the milk. You did it on purpose so that you could lick up the milk!'

The cat walked haughtily to the door, stood by it, miaowed, and looked round at Twiddle.

'Ha! Now you're ordering me to open the door, are you?' said Twiddle. 'Well, I won't. I've had enough of you, see? I shall not open another window or door for you all my life long!'

The cat sat down patiently by the door and began to wash itself again. Twiddle went on muttering. The kettle began to boil on the stove. Twiddle ran to take it off before it dripped all over the place.

The cat ran, too, and tripped up Twiddle as neatly as could be.

Down he went with the kettle and a tiny drop of the scalding water went over the cat. She set up

such a hullabaloo that Mrs Twiddle came rushing into the kitchen.

She was just in time to see Twiddle give the cat a most resounding whack. She was horrified.

'TWIDDLE! What are you doing to MY cat? I saw you smack it – and oh, poor thing, it must have got its tail scalded by the hot water!'

'It's been licking itself all morning,' said Twiddle. 'What about *me*? I've scalded myself, too – look, on my hand. That cat tripped me up on purpose to make me spill the water. Yes, I smacked it – and if it sits and looks at me like that I'll smack it again!'

'TWIDDLE!' cried Mrs Twiddle, amazed. 'This isn't like you. You sound so hard and horrid.'

'I *feel* hard and horrid,' said poor Twiddle, holding his scalded hand. 'I hope I've done the cat a lot of good, giving her a good smack like that. For two pins I'd give her another.'

'Now, stop, Twiddle,' said his wife, getting very stern. 'It doesn't do her any good to smack her.'

'How do you know?' said Twiddle. 'You've never smacked her. I tell you smacking is what she wants. I tell you smacking will make a different cat of her.'

'Well, it won't,' said Mrs Twiddle. 'It will just make her hate and hate you, Twiddle. You're very unkind indeed. That poor cat will never go near you again.'

'Well, that will be a very good thing,' said Twiddle. 'All the same I still say that smack has done her good.'

Mrs Twiddle was cross with him. She put on what Twiddle called her 'haughty face' and he didn't like it a bit. 'She keeps looking at me as if I was something on the rubbish heap,' he grumbled to himself. 'Oh dear, how long is she going to keep this up? It will make me miserable.'

The cat didn't go near Twiddle. It kept round Mrs Twiddle and mewed pitifully. Twiddle knew it was just making a fuss. Mrs Twiddle gave it all kinds of titbits and petted it and fussed it till poor Twiddle nearly went mad. Had that smack done it any good after all? If only it had!

Mrs Twiddle was so cold to poor Twiddle all day long that he really couldn't bear it. He very nearly said he was sorry he had been unkind to the cat, and only just stopped himself in time.

Then an idea came to him. It was a very silly idea, but still it *was* an idea. Mr Twiddle put on his coat and hat and called to his wife.

'Just going to get an evening paper, wife!'

And off he went. He bought the paper and then he went to the fishmonger's, where he bought a pound of yesterday's fish. It wasn't very fresh and the fish-monger was rather surprised at Twiddle picking out stale fish. Still, he didn't mind selling it, so off went Twiddle, the fish under his arm.

When he got to the field not far from his home, Mr Twiddle began to act in a most peculiar manner. He stepped into the field, looked cautiously round to make sure no one was watching him, and undid the parcel of stale fish. He spread it on the grass and then stamped on it! How he stamped! He jumped up and down on it too, and he even wiped the fish paper round his boots.

'There!' said Twiddle, walking out of the field and leaving the stale, jumped-on fish behind. 'Now if that cat doesn't follow me round like a shadow all this evening I shall be very surprised! Ha! Mrs Twiddle said the cat would never come near me again – but she will!'

He went in at the back door. Mrs Twiddle was in the kitchen, sweeping up some crumbs. The cat was sitting haughtily in the scullery. It gave Twiddle a very nasty look.

Twiddle walked in boldly, and pretended to aim a kick at the cat. It caught a whiff of the fishy smell on his boots, and opened its eyes wide. It sat up straight. My, what a wonderful smell!

Twiddle walked through into the kitchen. The cat followed at once, sniffing eagerly. It came right to Twiddle's heels. Mrs Twiddle looked up, still with her 'haughty face'. She was surprised to see the cat following Twiddle so closely.

'Nice and cosy in here, wife,' said Twiddle, amiably. 'I'll just hang my things in the hall.'

He went into the hall. The cat followed closely at his heels and came back at his heels, too, feeling excited. Twiddle had never smelt so nice before. Where *had* he been, thought the cat.

Twiddle walked through the kitchen and into the scullery, just to let his wife see the cat following him again. Mrs Twiddle said nothing, but she couldn't help feeling more and more astonished. She knew her cat. It was a touchy cat. Even a cross word made it sulk, and it never had liked Mr Twiddle, who was very free with his cross words at times.

'I'm just going to get the wood in for the morning,' said Twiddle, and he walked out into the garden. The cat followed him, almost bumping its nose into his heels.

'Call your cat,' said Twiddle, stopping so suddenly that the cat *did* bump its nose. 'It's better in the warm kitchen, wife.'

'Puss, Puss!' called Mrs Twiddle. 'Come to me, Puss dear.'

Puss-dear took not the slightest notice. She began

160

to purr round Twiddle, and even rubbed her head against his legs. Mrs Twiddle simply couldn't understand it.

'PUSS!' she called sharply. She didn't like the cat not coming to her when it was called. The cat gave her a sour look, and went on purring round Twiddle.

'Oh well, if she wants to be my shadow, let her!' said Twiddle airily, and went to the woodshed, followed by the cat.

He came back with the cat. He went upstairs and the cat went too. He went to wash his hands in the bathroom and when Mrs Twiddle popped her head round the door, there was the cat, almost sitting on Twiddle's feet.

Twiddle came into the kitchen with the purring cat. He sat down in his chair. 'Now,' he said sternly to the cat, 'I do *not* want you on my knee. I am still not pleased with you. Just remember that hard smack I gave you this morning, and behave yourself!'

The cat didn't attempt to jump up as she usually did. She sat down contentedly at Twiddle's feet, so

that the fishy smell on his boots kept coming to her
nose. She suddenly turned her head and began to
lick his boots with her pink tongue.

Mrs Twiddle was ironing and watching all the
time. She put down her iron. 'Twiddle,' she said, in
a much nicer voice than she had spoken to him all
day, 'Twiddle, look at that cat – it's licking your
boots!'

'Yes, I know. It's learnt that I'm master at last,'
said Twiddle comfortably. 'I told you that a smack
would do it good. It knows it's got to mind its p's
and q's with me now. Any more nonsense from it
and it will get another smack.'

Mrs Twiddle didn't say a word to that. She was
thinking very hard. She had never seen the cat so
attached to Twiddle before. Why, Twiddle might be
its best friend instead of someone who had scalded it

and smacked it not very many hours ago! Could it be that Twiddle was right? Did it need a good smack sometimes?

She went on ironing. The cat licked Twiddle's boots a bit longer, then lay down on his feet and went to sleep.

Mrs Twiddle simply could not get over its behaviour.

'Twiddle,' she said, after a bit, 'there's a funny sort of smell in this kitchen, isn't there? Sort of fishy smell.'

'Nonsense, my dear!' said Twiddle at once. 'Drains, I expect. You're always imagining things.'

'I hope the cat hasn't had the fish out of the larder,' said Mrs Twiddle, and she went to look. 'If she has I shall give her a good smack!'

That was too much for Mr Twiddle. He burst into such a loud laugh that the cat nearly jumped out of its skin. 'That's right, wife,' said Twiddle. 'I tell you, this cat is all the better for a good smack!'

He went out to post a letter, later on, not because he wanted to, but because he meant to show Mrs Twiddle that the cat would even go out to walk with him. It did, of course, keeping to his heels like a shadow again. Mrs Twiddle was most impressed.

Twiddle sat down again when he got in. 'Here are your slippers, Twiddle dear,' said Mrs Twiddle, in a meek voice, when he came in. 'I've warmed them for you.'

Twiddle was about to take them when he remembered not to. It would never do to take off his fishy boots – the cat would desert him at once! 'Can't be bothered to put on my slippers,' he said, much to Mrs Twiddle's astonishment. Really, what with Twiddle's behaviour and the cat's, she felt quite bewildered!

'Now, listen, wife. I won't have the cat wandering up into our bedroom tonight,' said Twiddle, sternly, when he and his wife were ready to go to bed. 'I'm tired of her sleeping on my middle. I can't think why she never sleeps on yours. She must stay down here in the scullery.'

'She won't,' said Mrs Twiddle.

'She will,' said Twiddle. He took off his boots and took them into the scullery. He stood them by the door to clean them in the morning. Then he spoke sternly to the cat.

'Cat! Sit down there by my boots and don't stir from them all night long. Do you hear?'

'Miaow,' said the cat, obediently, and lay down as close to the fishy boots as she possibly could. Mrs Twiddle could hardly believe her eyes.

'I think you're rather a wonderful man, Twiddle,' she said, when they went upstairs. 'Honestly, I never saw the cat so well-behaved – why, it was just like your shadow.'

'Well, just you be firm with it,' said Twiddle. 'And mind you back me up when it annoys me. Next time it trips me up and I smack it, you must smack it, too.'

'Oh, I think one smack would be enough,' said kind Mrs Twiddle. 'Well, well, to think of that cat adoring you all evening like that! Who would have thought it? I feel quite jealous!'

'Oh, it will stop bothering itself about me tomorrow,' said Mr Twiddle, getting into bed, 'and it will follow you around just as usual. You'll see!'

It will, of course, because old Twiddle will have cleaned his boots and they won't smell fishy any more!

The thing is, he sometimes forgets to clean them, and if Mrs Twiddle happens to do them for him, *what* will she think of the fishy smell? Twiddle, be sure you don't forget!

10

Mrs Twiddle's umbrella

'I'm just going out to fetch my paper,' Mr Twiddle called to Mrs Twiddle. 'I won't be long.'

'Take your umbrella, then, because it's raining hard,' called back Mrs Twiddle.

Twiddle looked for his umbrella. He couldn't find it anywhere. It wasn't in the hall stand, it wasn't hanging up with his coat, it wasn't upstairs in his bedroom.

'That tiresome umbrella!' muttered Mr Twiddle to himself. 'It's always disappearing. Could I have left it anywhere, I wonder?'

He thought hard. He might have left it at the post office. He might have left it at the butcher's. He might have left it at the fishmonger's. There were any amount of places where he had already left it at one time or another, and might have left it again the last time it rained.

Twiddle felt guilty. Mrs Twiddle always had a lot to say when he couldn't find his umbrella. She would make him go and ask at every shop in the town if she knew it wasn't in the hall stand.

'Haven't you gone yet?' called Mrs Twiddle. 'Do go, dear. I want you back in good time for dinner, you know. And bring back some fish for the cat, will you?'

'All right,' called Twiddle. 'Though I don't know why that cat should have so much fish. It has far more than we do. And I do hate carrying fish home on a wet day. It smells so, and—'

'Now, Twiddle, take a basket and go,' called Mrs Twiddle. 'Do you want me to come and button your coat and find your hat and put up your umbrella for you? Really, if I don't you'll never get away this morning.'

Twiddle looked once more at the hall stand in despair. Where, oh where was his tiresome umbrella? He heard Mrs Twiddle coming, and he snatched at the only umbrella in the stand. It belonged to Mrs Twiddle. Never mind, he would borrow it just this once.

He rushed out of the front door and banged it behind him. He buttoned his coat and put up his umbrella as he went down the path, afraid that Mrs Twiddle might call him back. She would be very cross if she knew he couldn't find his own umbrella and had taken hers.

Mr Twiddle went to get his paper. He stuffed it into his pocket because he didn't want it to get wet. Then he actually remembered to call at the fish shop for some fish for the cat. Twiddle didn't like his wife's cat. It always sat just where he could fall over it.

The fishmonger stuffed some fish heads and fish-tails into a bit of paper. Mr Twiddle took the parcel in disgust. Why hadn't he brought a basket as Mrs Twiddle had suggested? Now, his hands would smell of fish all day.

He put up his umbrella again and walked off down the street. Somebody called to him: 'Hey, Mr Twiddle! The sun is out and the rain's stopped. Why have you got your umbrella up?'

Twiddle stopped at once, feeling very foolish. Yes, it is a lovely sunny morning now, and he hadn't noticed. He tried to put the umbrella down with one hand, because he had the fish in the other, but he couldn't. It was too stiff. So he put the fish on a wall

for a moment and then managed to put the umbrella down.

'Meeow!' said a delighted voice, and a big tabby cat jumped up beside the fish. It tore at the bit of paper that wrapped it.

'Stop that!' said Twiddle, crossly, and gave the cat a whack with his umbrella. It yowled, and disappeared, taking with it the bit of paper the fish had been wrapped in.

'Bother!' said Twiddle annoyed. 'Now the fish hasn't got any paper – look at all the heads and tails slithering about on the wall. I can't carry them like that.'

He remembered his own newspaper safely stuffed in his pocket. He'd have to wrap the fish in that. How horrid! Still, there was nothing else to be done.

Twiddle carefully hooked his wife's umbrella in the branch of a tree that hung down over the wall. He wrapped the fish scraps in his paper, and walked off down the street.

He left his wife's umbrella behind him, of course. He never once thought of it until the rain suddenly began to fall again. Then he found he hadn't an umbrella to put up!

'Oh my! I hooked it on to that branch by the wall where I wrapped up the fish in my paper,' he groaned, and rushed back to get it.

But it wasn't there. Not a sign of an umbrella could he see! He called out to the woman in the little sweet shop opposite.

'Did you see anyone take an umbrella from this branch here? I left it not long ago.'

'Oh, yes,' called back the sweet-shop woman. 'Somebody took it not five minutes ago.'

'The thief!' said Twiddle, indignantly. 'What was he like?'

'It wasn't a he, it was a she,' said the woman. 'It was somebody dressed in a blue mackintosh and a hat with daisies on. She was rather plump, and hurried along like anything.'

'Thank you!' called Twiddle. 'I'll track down that nasty woman if it takes me all morning!'

So off he went, hunting for a plump woman in a blue mackintosh and a hat with daisies on it. He couldn't see her anywhere. He stopped a man on a corner and asked him if he had seen anyone dressed like that.

'Yes,' said the man. 'She passed me at the bottom of that road. She was going towards the bicycle shop, if you know where that is.'

Twiddle did. He raced along to the bicycle shop, getting wetter and wetter as the rain poured down. He felt very angry indeed. To think that that thief of a woman should steal his wife's umbrella and send him on a goose chase like this in the pouring rain.

He went into the shop. 'Did somebody wearing a blue mackintosh and a hat with daisies on come in here?' he asked. 'Somebody with a very nice umbrella – with a dog's head on the crook handle?'

'Yes,' said the boy there. 'She did. She said she was going down to the baker's – you might get her there.'

Off went Twiddle to the baker's. He peered inside. Nobody there at all. 'What do you want?' called the baker's wife.

'Somebody in a blue mackintosh and a hat with daisies,' called Twiddle in despair.

'Oh, she came in for a cake just now,' said the woman. 'She's only just gone. Hurry round the corner and you'll catch her!'

Twiddle hurried – ah, there was somebody in a blue mackintosh and hat with daisies, scurrying along with an umbrella up – his wife's umbrella, too! How dared the woman be such a thief! She deserved to go to prison.

At that very moment Mr Plod, the policeman, came round a corner and nearly bumped into Twiddle.

'Morning, Mr Twiddle,' said Mr Plod. 'How wet you are! I thought only policemen had to go out in the rain without umbrellas!'

'Mr Plod, you're just the man I want,' said Twiddle, eagerly. 'Someone's stolen my wife's umbrella, and the thief is there – look, down the road in front of us – with the very umbrella! What shall I do?'

'*I'll* deal with this,' said Mr Plod. 'That's what policemen are for. Come along with me, sir.'

So Mr Plod and Mr Twiddle hurried after the thief

in the blue mackintosh. Aha! She would soon be very frightened indeed.

'There – she's gone into Mrs Chatter's house.' said Mr Plod. 'We'll have to go and knock at the door and get in and face her. Come along.'

Mr Plod knocked loudly at the door. Mrs Chatter opened it and Mr Plod walked in.

Mr Twiddle stayed at the front door. He thought he would let Mr Plod deal with this. He heard the policeman's rumbling voice.

'I've had a report that an umbrella has been stolen,' he said. 'Was it you, madam, who took it?'

A voice answered him indignantly. 'Yes, it *was* me – and why shouldn't I take it? It was my own umbrella! There it was, hanging on the branch of a tree in the middle of the village street – *my* umbrella!

I'd like to know who put it there! Just wait till I find out who took my umbrella and hung it on a tree in the village street!'

'Dear me,' said Mr Plod. 'Are you *sure* it was your umbrella? What is your name, madam?'

'You know my name quite well – I'm Mrs Twiddle!' said the voice indignantly.

Well, Mr Twiddle could have told Mr Plod that, of course. He knew his wife's voice very well indeed. He stood shivering at the front door, feeling very upset indeed.

'You wait till Mr Twiddle hears about this,' went on Mrs Twiddle. 'He went out this morning with his own umbrella – and a little later I remembered I had to go out too. But I couldn't find my umbrella at all, so I put on my oldest hat and my mackintosh and out I went without one. And just IMAGINE how astonished I was suddenly to see my very own umbrella hanging on a tree in the village street! I couldn't believe my eyes.'

'Very strange,' agreed the policeman, wondering what Mr Twiddle was going to say about all this.

'And now you come banging at my friend's door and tell me somebody says I've stolen my own umbrella!' went on Mrs Twiddle. 'I never heard anything like it. Show me the person who says I stole it, and I'll show you the thief—it must be he who took my umbrella and hung it on that tree! He must be mad. He must be. . . .'

Twiddle didn't wait to hear any more. Feeling very sick indeed, he stole off down the path. He hoped Mr Plod wouldn't give him away. If only he could get home before Mrs Twiddle discovered anything more!

Mr Plod didn't give him away. He apologised to Mrs Twiddle and went off in a hurry before she could

ask him any awkward questions. Mrs Twiddle went home with her umbrella, very cross indeed.

Twiddle had got there first. He had opened the front door and had fallen over the cat, who, as usual, loved to sit in the very middle of the dark hall.

The cat sniffed at him. He smelt very pleasantly of fish. Twiddle felt about for the fish he had bought.

But he hadn't got it. He had left it on the wall when he had gone back to look for the umbrella!

'If you think I'm going back there to look for your fish, you're mistaken, Cat,' he said. But then he remembered that his morning paper was round the fish – and he wouldn't be able to read the news if he didn't get the fish!

He groaned and went to the front door again, followed by the excited cat.

He peered out. It was pouring with rain. He stepped out valiantly into it – and bumped into Mrs Twiddle hurrying down the path with her umbrella up.

'Twiddle, you're not going out again, are you?' she cried. 'I've got such a lot to tell you. Why are you going out again?'

'I've forgotten the cat's fish,' said Twiddle, desperately.

'Oh, never mind for once,' said Mrs Twiddle, anxious to tell Twiddle the story of her umbrella and Mr Plod.

'I *must* go and get it,' said Twiddle and shook himself away from his wife.

'Oh, Twiddle, it's very kind of you, but the cat can go without for once!' cried Mrs Twiddle. 'Come back. Where's your umbrella?'

'I don't know,' said Twiddle, in despair.

'But, Twiddle, you went out with your umbrella this morning – I saw you!' cried Mrs Twiddle. 'Oh,

Twiddle, have you lost it *again*? Did you come home without it? Here, take mine.'

'No, NO, NO!' shouted Twiddle, who felt that he could never touch his wife's umbrella again. 'I'd rather get soaked!'

And off went poor old Twiddle into the rain to get back the fish and his paper. But the tabby cat had been there before him, so he won't find either. Really, he is a most unlucky fellow, isn't he?

11

When Mr Twiddle was asleep

'I don't know when I've felt so sleepy,' said Mr Twiddle, yawning, one afternoon.

'You always do feel sleepy in the afternoon,' said Mrs Twiddle, bustling round. 'And you always say exactly what you've just said. Now, Twiddle, I'm going out to see old Mrs Tabbit. You stay here in case anyone comes to the door.'

'Right!' said Twiddle, pleased at the idea of a peaceful afternoon in front of the fire. 'Is anyone likely to come?'

'No,' said Mrs Twiddle. 'And, Twiddle, see that the door is kept shut, will you, so that the cat doesn't get in and wander round. She'll try to get my knitting if she can. She's been a naughty puss lately over that.'

'I'll be very pleased to keep the cat out,' said Twiddle, settling down in his chair and opening his newspaper. 'Nothing I should like better. The longer she's out the more I'll be pleased.'

Mrs Twiddle put on her hat and coat and said goodbye. 'Now have a good snooze,' she said. 'You really do look rather tired – been reading the newspaper too much, I expect! Goodbye, Twiddle dear.'

'Goodbye, my love,' said Twiddle, feeling very amiable indeed. Fancy having an afternoon with nobody telling him to do this, that and the other – and the cat forbidden to come in, too! Now she wouldn't be able to sit herself on his knee all the afternoon and dig her claws into him. Aha! this was wonderful.

He was asleep before Mrs Twiddle had passed by the window. She had a look in and smiled to herself. 'Poor old Twiddle – he really *is* tired today!' she thought. 'I do hope nothing disturbs him.'

She went on her way to Mrs Tabbit's. Halfway there she met Mr Screw, the carpenter. He nodded to her.

'You naughty man!' said Mrs Twiddle, playfully. 'You haven't been to do the lock of my kitchen door yet – and it *is* so difficult to lock.'

'Well, there, ma'am – if I hadn't forgotten all about it!' said Mr Screw. He was a great big man, with a shock of red hair and a big nose. 'I'm right down sorry. Look, I've got a bit of time this afternoon. I'll go right along and do it now.'

'Oh, that *would* be nice of you,' said Mrs Twiddle. 'Could you really? The only thing is – you'll disturb Mr Twiddle. He's asleep in the kitchen and really very tired.'

'He sleeps so soundly that he won't hear *me*,' said Mr Screw. 'I'll be very quiet, ma'am. He won't know I've been.'

So off he hurried to Twiddle's house. He was soon there. He peeped in at the kitchen window and saw Twiddle fast asleep. He went to the door and opened it.

He examined the lock. Dear, dear, he hadn't got the right tools with him – and if he tried to do it without them he would probably make a tremendous noise, and that would wake up Mr Twiddle.

Mr Screw scratched his head. If he went to fetch the right tools, and came back again, he'd be late for his next job. What could he do? Perhaps he had

better make a noise after all and chance waking up
Mr Twiddle?

'No, I won't do that,' said the carpenter, suddenly.
'I know a better idea. 'I'll simply take the door off its
hinges and carry it home with me – do the lock there
and carry the door back. It won't take me any time
then.'

So, very quietly, he began to take the door off its
hinges. The cat came and watched him with much
interest. She hadn't seen a door taken off before. She
was pleased. Now she could get into the warm
kitchen and perhaps find something to eat.

'Miaow!' said the cat and rubbed herself against
the carpenter.

'Sh!' said the carpenter. 'You'll wake Mr Twiddle.'

The cat didn't mind about that at all, and went on miaowing. But Twiddle didn't stir. He was fast asleep and dreaming a wonderful dream about a dish of fried steak and onions that never grew smaller however much he ate of it. He snored a little.

Soon the carpenter had the door right off. He lifted it up on his shoulder and went off with it. The cat shot into the room as soon as the doorway was empty and leapt on to Twiddle's knee, digging her claws into him as usual.

Twiddle woke up with a jump. He stared at the cat in anger. 'How did *you* get in?' he asked, exasperated. 'Door and window shut and yet you appear. Get down from my knee at once.'

'Miaow,' said the cat and tried to rub her head against Twiddle's chin. That was too much. He put her down and shut his eyes again. 'I don't know how you got in, but you can go out the same way,' he said.

An icy draught blew round his chair. Twiddle sat up and looked at the fire. Had it gone down while he was asleep? Why was the room so cold?

No, the fire was beautiful. He sat back again and shut his eyes. But a little wind lifted his hair at the top, where it showed above the chair. Twiddle was puzzled. *Where* was this frightful draught coming from?

He looked round his chair – and to his enormous surprise, he saw the empty doorway. The wind was blowing through and making the place as cold as could be.

Twiddle didn't notice that the door was gone at first – he simply thought it was wide open. He glared at the cat. 'Did *you* manage to open that door on your own, you maddening, tiresome cat?'

The cat said nothing but began to wash herself. Twiddle got up and went to shut the door.

But the door, of course, wasn't there. Twiddle stared as if he couldn't believe his eyes. He ran his hand round the doorway – no, there was no door at all. It had absolutely vanished!

'Well – I must still be asleep, that's all,' said Twiddle, bewildered. 'I'll go and sit down again and maybe the door will be back again when I next wake up.'

So he went and sat down again – but he was so puzzled that he couldn't go to sleep. He kept looking round his chair at the empty doorway, and shivering in the draught.

'Somebody must have stolen the door!' he said to himself at last. 'A thief must have crept up when I was asleep, and taken the door off – the wicked robber!'

He went into the garden and called his next-door neighbour. 'Hey! Did you see a man carrying a door this afternoon?'

The neighbour stared. 'No. Why should I? People don't usually go about carrying doors.'

'Well, *someone* is going about carrying a door,' said Twiddle, suddenly feeling very fierce indeed, 'and what's more I'm going to find out who it is!'

He rushed indoors, fell over the cat, got his hat and stick and rushed out. He trotted into the town, looking everywhere for a man carrying a door. But there wasn't one to be seen anywhere. This wasn't surprising, because the carpenter was now busily mending the lock in his own workroom.

As soon as he had finished it, he popped the door on his shoulder again and off he went back to Mr Twiddle's house. By that time Twiddle was at the other end of the town, walking up the steps to the police station, looking very fierce indeed.

'What do you want, sir?' asked the constable there.

'Someone's stolen my door!' said Twiddle, and he banged his hand on the desk. 'I want it back!'

'What door?' asked the policeman, astonished.

'My kitchen door,' said Mr Twiddle. 'When I was fast asleep, too. Taken it right away.'

'Er – well – this is very peculiar,' said the constable, and reached for his helmet. 'I'll come with you and make a report, sir.'

Twiddle marched him all the way to his house. He went down the back path to the kitchen door. 'This is where the door was stolen,' he said and stopped suddenly.

The door was back! There it was, fast shut, and looking very solid indeed. Mr Screw had put it back five minutes before and had then gone off again.

The policeman stared stolidly at the door. 'You playing a joke on me?' he enquired.

Mr Twiddle looked scared. He felt the door gingerly. It was real and solid – but when he had left the house it hadn't been there. Now it was back! He simply couldn't understand it!

'Er – very peculiar,' said Mr Twiddle, still staring at the door. 'It wasn't there when I left. Now it's come back.'

'Doors don't come and go like that,' said the constable, putting away his notebook. 'I don't suppose you took a good look, sir – the door must have been there all the time. Good afternoon.'

Mrs Twiddle came in at that moment and was most surprised to see a policeman going out of the back gate. She hurried up to Twiddle, who was still standing outside the back door, looking puzzled.

'Twiddle, what have you been up to? Why did that policeman call?' she panted.

'Well – er – it was nothing much,' said Twiddle, suddenly feeling that he didn't really want to discuss vanishing doors with Mrs Twiddle. He didn't feel that she would believe him. 'He – er – well, he just came about a door.'

'About a *door*!' said Mrs Twiddle, even more astonished. 'What door?'

She opened the kitchen door and went inside. The very first thing she saw was the cat playing with her knitting! It had rolled the ball of wool all over the place, and had undone half the jumper she was making. Now it was busy chewing her needles!

She gave a scream. 'Oh, you wicked cat! Give her a smack, quick, Twiddle!'

Twiddle was only too pleased. He smacked hard at the cat, which dodged aside, and Twiddle hit his hand hard against the dresser. The cat fled out of the open door.

'*You* deserve a smack, too, Twiddle,' said Mrs Twiddle, angrily. 'Didn't I *ask* you not to let the cat in?'

'I didn't let her in,' said Twiddle, sucking his hand.

'Well, you must have done. She can't come in through a shut door,' said Mrs Twiddle.

'She did,' said Twiddle. 'But wait a minute – perhaps she didn't. Perhaps she came in after the door had gone!'

'Gone?' said Mrs Twiddle, staring at Twiddle. '*Gone?* What do you mean – *gone?* Doors don't go.'

'This one did,' said Twiddle; 'I fetched the police about it. And when we came back, the door had come again.'

'Twiddle, dear, do you feel quite well?' said Mrs Twiddle, suddenly, thinking he must be going mad or something. 'Would you like to go to bed?'

Twiddle thought it would be a good idea. Then perhaps he wouldn't have to do any more explaining about cats and knitting and doors that came and went.

'I think I *will* go to bed,' said Twiddle. So up he went. Mrs Twiddle fussed over him like anything. She gave him a hot-water bottle, she brought him hot milk, she even went out to buy him a late newspaper. He was tremendously pleased. He really enjoyed himself.

He's never found out why the door came and went, because the carpenter didn't bother to tell Mrs

Twiddle about it. Mr Twiddle would have forgotten all about it long ago, if it wasn't that he keeps meeting the policeman he fetched that day.

''Morning, Mr Twiddle,' the policeman says each time. 'Had any more trouble with your *doors*?'

Dear old Twiddle! I can't help liking him; can you?

12

Twiddle goes for a walk

Mrs Twiddle bustled in just at teatime. It was a winter's evening, and already almost dark outside. She called Twiddle.

'Twiddle! Twiddle! Where are you? Have you got the tea ready as I told you?'

Twiddle hadn't. He had gone to sleep in front of the kitchen fire, and had only just woken up when he heard Mrs Twiddle come in. He was now scurrying round filling the kettle, putting it on the stove, and trying to get out all the tea things at once!

'Twiddle! Can't you hear me? I'm home!' called Mrs Twiddle, walking into the kitchen. 'Dear me – you haven't even got the tea laid.'

'Just ready, *just* ready!' said Twiddle, banging the loaf down on the platter. 'You must be early, my dear.'

'No, I'm not!' said Mrs Twiddle, taking off her hat. 'I'm late. And I'm tired and thirsty. I suppose you slept in front of the kitchen fire from the moment I went out and shut the door to the moment I came back, Twiddle. And I suppose you haven't done a single thing I asked you to – not one!'

Twiddle fell over the cat and didn't answer. He glared at the cat. 'Did you do that on purpose, you miserable animal? How did you get in? You were outside when I began to get tea.'

'Oh, Twiddle – she must have got in through the

bedroom window,' said Mrs Twiddle. 'And I *asked*
you to be sure and shut it if it rained. You can't have
shut it. Did you?'

As Twiddle hadn't even known it had been raining
that afternoon he certainly hadn't shut the window.
Trust that cat to give him away!

'And did you fetch in some more coal as I asked
you?' asked Mrs Twiddle. 'Oh, dear – no, you didn't!
The scuttle is empty. And did you take the clothes in
off the line? Oh, *Twiddle* – they're still there. I can see
them flapping in the darkness. They'll be soaked
with the rain! And what about the dog? Did you take
him for a short walk?'

Twiddle hadn't done anything at all except go to
sleep. He felt very much ashamed of himself. Dear,
dear – he hadn't even *thought* about the dog!

'Oh, Twiddle – I do think you are very very mean,'

said poor Mrs Twiddle, sitting down. 'I've been busy all the afternoon nursing my poor sister, and I did so want my tea ready when I got home. I don't believe you love me one bit. Not one bit. You haven't done a thing I asked you.'

To Twiddle's horror she burst into tears. He hurried over with his big hanky, but she pushed him away.

'No! You don't love me!' she sobbed. 'I know you don't. You just went to sleep and forgot all about me.'

Twiddle felt very guilty indeed. He felt lazy and unkind and selfish and good-for-nothing. He tried again to dry his wife's eyes. But she wouldn't let him. Twiddle was very miserable.

What could he do to put things right? He rushed about, made the tea, cut bread and butter and put out cakes. He tore out into the darkness and brought in the clothes from the line. He fell over the cat again, and didn't say a word. He rushed upstairs and shut the bedroom window, because it was raining once more. He went out and got some more coal in. The cat went with him, very interested in Twiddle's sudden fit of hurry-scurry.

He nearly fell over her again. He didn't say a word but pushed her into the coal cellar and shut the door firmly. 'You'll be out of my way in there,' he whispered, when he had banged the door. The cat settled down on the coal and began to wash herself. She quite liked the coal cellar.

But still Mrs Twiddle wouldn't forgive poor Twiddle. She ate her tea in silence. She wouldn't look at him. It was really dreadful.

Twiddle couldn't eat anything, he was so upset. What else could he do to show his little wife that he was very sorry? He sat and thought. Then he got up and took down his hat and coat. 'I'm going to take

the poor dog for a run,' he said. 'I'll fetch him from his kennel.'

The rain was pelting against the windows, and Twiddle did hope that Mrs Twiddle would say no, he wasn't to go out in such a downpour. But she didn't. She just sat and drank her tea and wouldn't even *look* at poor Twiddle! So out he went into the rain and darkness, and made his way to the kennel.

Rain or not, the dog was very glad to see him. He would hardly stand still for Twiddle to put on his lead. In the end Twiddle dropped it on the ground and couldn't find it again in the darkness. Oh, dear! He really didn't want to go back into the house to get a torch to look for the lead. So he took a bit of rope and tied that through the dog's collar instead.

He set off with the dog in the rain. He hadn't got an umbrella, so he soon got wet. He was hungry and thirsty because he hadn't had any tea. He was also very miserable. So was the dog, because he didn't think walks in the rain and darkness were much fun – and he didn't like a silent, unhappy master.

Twiddle soon came to the town. He came to a brightly lit little place called 'Tilly's Tearoom'. A nice smell of toast came out from the door. It made Mr Twiddle feel very hungry indeed. He knew this tearoom. It was a place where farmers came after market to have tea and toast and new-baked ginger cake. Outside was a strong railing to which they could tie their horses, cows, a sheep or two, and dogs.

Twiddle decided to go in and have some tea and toast. He tied the dog firmly to the railings by his rope. 'Shan't be long, old fellow,' he said. 'It's stopped raining now so you'll be all right.'

Twiddle enjoyed his tea and toast and new ginger cake. Then he thought he had better be getting back because Mrs Twiddle might think he was out too long. So he paid his bill and got up to go.

It was pitch dark outside now. Twiddle wished and wished he had brought a torch. He groped his way to the railings and fell over what seemed to be a pig, by its excited grunts. He felt about for his dog.

'Where are you?' he said, and the dog barked gladly. Twiddle undid the rope from the railing and set off home.

'Come along,' he said. 'We'll get back. I shall be glad of my warm fire and you'll be glad of your cosy kennel.'

He walked home quickly, glad that it had stopped raining. He took the dog to its kennel and shut it in, giving it a push because it didn't seem to want to go in. Then he went indoors, hoping that Mrs Twiddle was in a better temper now.

But she wasn't. 'Where's the cat?' she asked him. 'I can hear her yowling, but I can't find her.'

Twiddle remembered where she was – oh, dear, in the coal cellar! He went to the door and listened.

Yes – she was yowling loudly. Then he heard another noise, too – one that puzzled him.

'Hiss-ss-ss! Hiss-ss-ss-ss!'

'What in the world is *that* noise?' asked Mrs Twiddle, surprised.

'Sounds like a large snake, or something.'

'HISS-SS-SS-SS!'

'Whatever can it be?' said Mrs Twiddle stepping back quickly. 'Gracious – if there's an escaped snake in the garden I shall scream the place down.'

Twiddle was just about to shut the door when they heard another noise – a loud cackling, angry and fierce. Mrs Twiddle looked most alarmed.

'Why – is there a goose out in the garden with the snake?' she asked. 'Oh, Twiddle, dear Twiddle, I do feel frightened. Please do go and get the dog – he'll soon scare away any creatures that shouldn't be about.'

Twiddle was pleased to hear himself being called 'dear' again, but he didn't much like going out into the darkness among snakes and geese that seemed suddenly to have arrived from nowhere. The cat yowled loudly again.

'Let the cat in, too, wherever she is,' said Mrs Twiddle. 'Do go on, Twiddle. Aren't you brave enough?'

Twiddle didn't really think he was – but he didn't feel that he could possibly risk making Mrs Twiddle cross again, so out he went in the darkness, very valiantly.

He went to the coal cellar and let out the cat, which flew past him with a loud screech.

Then, hoping that he wouldn't tread on a hissing snake or bump into a fierce goose, he went to the dog's kennel. He thought that he would feel much better with the dog beside him. He opened the kennel door and called the dog.

'Come on, old fellow, come on!'

He felt a sharp pain in his hand and drew back, shocked. 'You bit me!' he said. 'You bad dog! You bit your own master! Come on out.'

But the dog wouldn't come out. Instead that peculiar hissing noise came again. Twiddle scurried away in terror.

'The snake's in the kennel with the dog – and the dog bit me!' he shouted to his wife. Mrs Twiddle was most astonished.

'The dog *bit* you!' she said. 'Our own dear gentle dog! I don't believe it. I shall go out at once with the torch and bring him in myself, snakes or no snakes!'

And out she went, shining the torch bravely in front of her. Twiddle followed her. They came to the kennel and Mrs Twiddle shone her torch in to see the dog. She gave such a loud cry of alarm and astonishment that Twiddle almost scuttled back to the house again.

'Twiddle! Look – what's this in our dog's kennel? Oh, TWIDDLE! IT'S A GOOSE!'

And sure enough an enormous goose poked out her head and cackled and hissed loudly at Mrs Twiddle. She pushed it back and shut the kennel door on it. She went back to the house with Twiddle, marvelling at the goose in the kennel.

'A goose! A *goose*! However did it get in the dog's kennel? And where is the dog? No wonder we thought there were snakes about when that goose hissed! Twiddle, did *you* put that goose into the kennel?'

Twiddle was just about to say no, of *course* not, how could he – when a dreadful thought came into his head.

Could he *possibly* have untied a goose from that railing, instead of his dog? It had been so dark that he might have got the ropes muddled and taken someone else's goose and left his poor old dog. Yes – he remembered now – the goose had felt very soft when he had pushed what he thought was his dog, into the kennel. It must have been a goose.

He had brought back somebody's goose! Oh dear, oh dear!

'Maybe I brought back a goose instead of the dog,' he said. 'I stopped and had tea at a tearoom and tied the dog up outside. Now don't you say a word, wife – I'll take back the goose and find our dog.'

So out went poor Twiddle into the rain and darkness again, pulling the surprised and angry goose behind him. How he hoped his dog was still there!

And at home Mrs Twiddle was staring angrily at

the cat, who was lying on a clean cushion making it absolutely black with coal dust from the coal cellar! Her paws and fur were black with it.

'And where have *you* been, I should like to know?' she said. 'Sitting in the cellar again, I suppose? How many times have I chased you out of there? You bad animal! Out you go and get yourself clean in the rain!'

And when Twiddle came home with the dog he was met by the cat, flying angrily out of the door with Mrs Twiddle chasing it. Twiddle was pleased. He never had liked his wife's cat.

'Bring the poor dog in and dry him. And dry yourself too, Twiddle,' said Mrs Twiddle in a kind voice. 'I'll make you some hot cocoa. That cat must have been in the coal cellar again! Just *look* at my nice clean cushion!'

Twiddle looked, but he didn't say a word. He wasn't going to risk making Mrs Twiddle cross all over again by explaining how the cat got into the coal cellar. It was nice to see her smiling once more. He and the dog could snuggle up peacefully together by the fire.

They did – and will you believe it, Twiddle is fast asleep again! And so is the dog.

13

Mr Twiddle and the dogs

'It's a very funny thing, Twiddle,' said Mrs Twiddle, 'but I always notice that if anyone ever brings a dog here, it never goes to *you*. It always makes a fuss of *me*.'

Mr Twiddle felt cross. 'It's merely because *you* make a fuss of the dog,' he said. 'Anyway, my love, you always make such a dreadful fuss of our cat that it has quite turned me against making a fuss of any creature, dog, cat or horse.'

'That's not the true reason,' said Mrs Twiddle, indignantly. 'You know perfectly well that cats don't like you, and dogs don't either. I don't think that's very nice, Twiddle. I think there must be something wrong with you.'

Mr Twiddle put down his newspaper. 'There's NOTHING wrong with me,' he said. 'I do like cats, but ours makes such a habit of tripping me up that I don't see why I should make a fuss of her. And I do like dogs, but, as I say, surely one person going crazy over any dog visitor is enough. I've no doubt all the dogs would come to me if you didn't make such a fuss of them that they don't even know I'm here!'

'Very well,' said Mrs Twiddle. 'Very well, Twiddle. The very next time any dog comes I will hardly take any notice of it at all – but you'll see, it will still come to me and not to you.'

'You are quite wrong, my love,' said Twiddle, and began to read his newspaper again.

'Now listen, Twiddle,' said Mrs Twiddle. 'I'm certain I'm right and you're certain I'm wrong. Very well – if I prove right you must give me a new hat. And if you prove right I'll give you a new scarf.'

Mr Twiddle didn't like the sound of that at all. He had a kind of feeling that all dogs would go fawning round dear, kind, plump little Mrs Twiddle. There was something about her that animals and children couldn't resist. He sighed.

'Why do you pester me so? Very well – I'll buy you a new hat if you're right. Now, do let me read my newspaper, and stop talking about dogs.'

Mr Twiddle didn't really think much more about all this till he saw his wife looking at a hat catalogue – and to his horror he noticed that she had put a cross beside a very pretty hat. Goodness gracious, it was three pounds and five shillings! Mr Twiddle began to feel alarmed.

'Suppose she makes me buy such a very expensive hat?' he thought. 'I wouldn't be able to buy any tobacco for my pipe for about three months. This will never do. I must think hard.'

So he thought hard for a day or two, and then he suddenly stopped looking worried. He felt that he knew what to do. So he went to the butcher and bought a nice threepenny bone that just fitted neatly into his right-hand trouser pocket without showing. He put it there, and patted it. Aha! Dogs would feel very friendly towards him now!

That very day his wife's sister came, bringing with her a little yappy poodle. 'Oh, the darling!' said Mrs Twiddle, and held out her hands to it.

It began to run to her – but halfway to Mrs Twiddle it stopped and sniffed. What was that

Perfectly Delicious Smell coming from over on the right, where that man was sitting with his newspaper? Sniff-Sniff! Lovely smell!

The dog dodged away from Mrs Twiddle and ran to Mr Twiddle. Ah – the smell was here! It leapt straight up on to Twiddle's knee and began to lick him.

'Well, I never!' said Mrs Twiddle, astonished. 'Look at that!'

Twiddle smiled broadly. He put the dog down. 'Go to Missus, then,' he said. 'Go to Missus and say how-de-do!'

But no – the dog only wanted to be near this exciting bone smell.

Where was it? It leapt up again on to Mr Twiddle and made a fuss of him.

'I'm afraid that's one up to you, Twiddle,' said Mrs Twiddle, surprised and not very pleased. 'What a very peculiar thing!'

'Not at all. Probably likes my smell,' said Twiddle truthfully, and pushed the dog away again.

The next day old Mrs Dally came in, bringing with her a rather muddy spaniel. 'Oh, the dear boy!' cooed Mrs Twiddle. 'The beautiful, long-eared boy!'

But the beautiful long-eared boy didn't give her even a glance. It gave one delightful sniff and flew to Mr Twiddle. Forty pounds of very muddy, rather smelly dog leapt on to his plump knees, and licked him vigorously from hair to chin. Mr Twiddle fended him off.

'Don't! Oooh, you're a very drippy dog. Take your tongue away from my nose. I've already washed my face once this morning. Go away, I tell you! You smell!'

'Funny that my darling doggy has taken such a fancy to your husband when he doesn't like dogs, isn't it?' said Mrs Dally, who wasn't pleased to hear her dog called smelly.

'It is queer,' agreed Mrs Twiddle, puzzled and rather upset. Could it be that Mr Twiddle really did attract dogs after all? Look at that spaniel now – snuffing all over him, sniff-snuff-sniffle-snuffle! Why, anyone would think it was his own dog!

The spaniel could smell the bone in Mr Twiddle's trouser pocket and was thrilled. It scrabbled and scraped at him, licking him and flapping its long ears about till Twiddle could bear it no longer. He rose suddenly from his chair and the dog fell to the floor.

'If there's one thing worse than a man making a silly fuss of a dog, it's a dog making a silly fuss of a man!' he said. 'Now, wife, perhaps you'll say I'm right and you're wrong – dogs do prefer me!'

'They certainly seem to,' said Mrs Twiddle. 'Oh dear – now I'll have to buy you the scarf and go without that dear little hat!'

Mr Twiddle looked at her. Well, if she was going to buy him a scarf, he *would* buy her a hat – but not that very expensive one – oh, no!

'Listen, my love,' he said. 'You can buy me the scarf, as I am right and you are wrong; but I'll buy *you* a hat, though *not* more than thirty shillings will I spend! Just to show you that I'm a kind and generous husband!'

'Oh, you are, you are!' cried Mrs Twiddle, and she ran to hug him. The spaniel leapt at them both, still trying to get to Mr Twiddle's trouser pocket. That bone! Oh, how good it smelt!

'Well, I *still* can't understand my doggy making a fuss of Mr Twiddle,' said Mrs Dally, annoyed. 'He's never done that before.'

Now, the next day, Mr and Mrs Twiddle set off to buy the scarf and the hat. They bought the scarf, a nice dark-blue one with white spots. Mr Twiddle fancied himself very much in it. Then they went off to the hat shop.

Now, on the way, who should they meet but little Mr Trot with his great big Alsatian dog. Mrs Twiddle always said she didn't know if Mr Trot was taking the dog for a walk, or if the dog was taking Mr Trot for one.

Mr Twiddle suddenly remembered the bone in his trouser pocket. He had forgotten to take it out! He began to cross the road in a hurry, before the Alsatian could smell it. But Mrs Twiddle pulled him back.

'We must have a word with Mr Trot, dear,' she said. 'And we *must* pat his lovely Alsatian.'

Mr Twiddle didn't want to do anything of the sort, but it was too late to retreat now. The great dog had already caught a whiff of the rather smelly bone. It bounded at Mr Twiddle with a bark of welcome and almost knocked him over. Little Mr Trot was pulled violently along on the lead.

'Get down, you brute! Hey, get down! Stop it! Don't poke me in the face with your clumsy paws!' yelled Mr Twiddle, sending the big dog away. But the Alsatian was certain that Mr Twiddle was a long-lost friend, a friend with a delicious bony smell, someone who would very soon produce the bone, if only the Alsatian could make a big enough fuss of him.

Mr Trot tugged at the lead. The dog took no notice. He leapt at Mr Twiddle again, his tongue out, and Mr Twiddle went down like a skittle. Bang! He was full-length on the pavement, squirming away from the excited dog.

Mrs Twiddle was absolutely astounded to see a dog making such a fuss of Twiddle – even knocking him over in his affection! Good gracious! But she didn't like to see Twiddle on the ground, so she poked the dog with her umbrella.

'Stop it, stop it! Let him get up!'

The Alsatian was worrying at Twiddle's right-hand trouser pocket. He tore it. He snapped at the bone there and pulled it out, together with Twiddle's handkerchief, a tobacco pouch and a ten-shilling note. WOOF! What a bone!

After that Mr Trot found it easy to manage his enormous dog. The Alsatian was quite willing to trot home quietly, with his smelly bone, and off he went, dragging his little master behind him.

Mrs Twiddle helped Twiddle up. She looked at him very crossly indeed. '*I* saw what you had in your pocket,' she said. 'A bone! You are a fraud, Twiddle. A great big shocking fraud! That's why the dogs made such a fuss of you – just because you put a bone in your pocket. I'm ashamed of you! You've got a new scarf out of me unfairly. You – you – you . . . oh dear, I'm going to cry!'

But Twiddle couldn't bear that. He put his arm round plump little Mrs Twiddle and gave her a squeeze.

'What are you crying for?' he said. 'It was just a silly joke. Come on – we're going to buy that three-pound-five-shilling hat. Cheer up!'

So Mrs Twiddle cheered up at once, and smiled happily. 'You're a very silly man,' she said. 'Very silly indeed. But sometimes I think you're quite nice. Oh, Twiddle, *don't* go putting bones in your pocket again – you've no idea how they will make your clothes smell!'

'You needn't worry. I shall never do that again,' said Twiddle, trotting along. 'You can have all the fussy dogs there are. I don't want ANY!'

14

Mr Twiddle gets a surprise

'I'm just going out, my love!' Mr Twiddle called to Mrs Twiddle.

'Twiddle! Now don't you forget the fish for the cat!' called Mrs Twiddle, running to the front door. 'And pay the bill at the newspaper shop. And goodness, don't you want a basket for the fish? You know how you make your coat smell if you come home clutching the packet of fish to your chest!'

'Dear me, yes – I must have a basket,' said Twiddle. His wife ran to get it. When she came back she had his mackintosh with her, too. 'It's going to rain,' she said. 'You had better take this, too, Twiddle.'

Twiddle set off, his mackintosh over one arm, and the basket swinging in his hand. He met Mr Grin and had a nice little talk with him. He met Miss Hurry, but she was gone before he could say more than 'Good morning.'

As he passed the cake shop a very nice smell of hot scones came out. Twiddle stopped and sniffed. 'I think I'll pop in and have a cup of hot coffee and a scone or two,' he thought. 'I really didn't have much breakfast.'

So in he went and chose a table. Soon he was sipping a cup of coffee and eating a whole plate of warm, buttered scones. Very nice, indeed!

He heard a noise outside and looked out of the

window. 'There now!' he said. 'Mrs Twiddle was right – it's raining! What a good thing I've got my mac. It's simply pouring down!'

He paid his bill, picked up his basket, and went to get his mac from the peg nearby. 'Now, let me see – what did I have to get?' he wondered. 'What *was* it now? Fish for breakfast? Fetch the papers? Call at the cleaners? What shopping did I have to do?'

He struggled into his mac and went out into the rain. Bother! What was it his wife had told him to get? The rain splashed into his face, and he groped in his pocket for a handkerchief.

He brought out a nice clean one, still folded tidily. Nice Mrs Twiddle! She had even put a clean hanky in his pocket for him! He felt something else there as well, and pulled it out.

Oh, *good*! A shopping list! Now he didn't need to try and remember what he had to get. Dear Mrs Twiddle had written it all down and he couldn't possibly make a mistake! He heaved a sigh of relief.

He put his hand in the other pocket and found his pipe there – and a small tin of his tobacco. How very, very kind of Mrs Twiddle. Mr Twiddle felt very loving towards her and made up his mind to buy her some roses. She was very fond of roses.

He lighted his pipe and looked at the list of shopping. It was rather a long one – no wonder Mrs Twiddle had written it all out, instead of leaving it to him to remember! Ha – herrings for breakfast – he *thought* there was something about fish! Toothpaste – cotton wool – he must go to the chemist for those. And what was this?

'Nice big bone,' read Twiddle. 'That's a bit funny. Oh, I expect she wants it for soup. Sausages – well, I can get those at the butcher's too. And, dear me – a *coal hammer*! Well, well – does Mrs Twiddle expect me to break up those big lumps of coal? She hasn't said a *word* to me about it!'

'Chocolate cake' came next on the list. Mr Twiddle beamed. He liked chocolate cake, and Mrs Twiddle hardly ever bought one because, she said, they were too dear. And look at this – six crumpets! If there was one thing Mr Twiddle liked more than another it was toasted crumpets for tea!

'No wonder Mrs Twiddle told me to take a basket,' he thought. 'Well, well – what a lot of shopping – but very *nice* shopping, I must say. Chocolate cake – crumpets – sausages. Well, I hope *those* are for supper.'

Twiddle went off happily, smoking his pipe. He must certainly remember to buy some roses for Mrs

Twiddle now. After all, she was going to give him such nice meals, she deserved some roses!

He went to the fishmonger's and bought some herrings. Ha, he would enjoy those! He went to the chemist and bought his favourite toothpaste and nice big packet of cotton wool.

When he came out of the chemist's shop he found it had stopped raining, so he took off his mac and folded it neatly over his arm.

'Now to the butcher for a big bone,' said Twiddle, quite enjoying himself. 'And the sausages, too. Look at them, all looped round the front of his shop.'

He came out of the butcher's shop with two big bones and a pound of pork sausages. Then he went off to the ironmonger's and bought a really fine coal hammer. 'This will break up those big lumps of coal quite easily!' he thought, and swung it up and down in the air.

'Now then, now then!' said a voice just behind him. 'You nearly hit me on the nose!'

It was Mr Surly, so Twiddle said he was very, very sorry, he was just trying out his coal hammer to see how it would break up big lumps of coal.

'You're lucky to *have* coal,' said Mr Surly. 'We've only got wood. And fancy having lumps big enough to break up! Where did you get them from?'

Mr Twiddle had no idea, and as he didn't at all like Mr Surly, he popped into the shop that sold crumpets and got rid of Mr Surly that way.

He bought the biggest chocolate cake he could see and six lovely crumpets with holes in them that made them look just like flat sponges.

By this time his basket was very, very full, and he staggered homewards with it.

Last of all he bought three beautiful red roses. 'Red roses mean "I love you",' said Twiddle to

himself, pleased. 'Aha! Mrs Twiddle will like those!'

He got home and went indoors. Mrs Twiddle was in the kitchen. Twiddle tiptoed into the sitting room, got a vase, filled it with water and put the three red roses into it. He left them in the middle of the table for Mrs Twiddle to see. He called her.

'I'm in the kitchen!' she cried. 'Just baking a cake. Come in here to me, Twiddle.'

Twiddle went in with his basket. 'I've done all the shopping,' he said. 'Quite a lot, too, there was.'

'Oh, no, Twiddle dear – there wasn't very much,' said Mrs Twiddle, busy at the oven.

'Meow,' said the cat, smelling the fish and coming over to rub herself against Mr Twiddle's legs.

'Don't,' said Twiddle. 'You make the ankles of my trousers all hairy. How many times have I told you not to do that, Cat?'

'I expect she smells the fish you've brought her,' said Mrs Twiddle, looking into her oven.

'Fish for the cat? You said herrings for breakfast!' said Twiddle, in alarm.

'I didn't!' said Mrs Twiddle. 'We've got kippers for breakfast. You bought them yourself yesterday. *Don't* say you've got herrings as well. Really, Twiddle! Did you pay the bill at the newspaper shop? I gave you the money for it.'

'Er – no. Dear me, that wasn't on the list,' said Twiddle, feeling muddled. 'Yes – I do remember your asking me now. But. . . .'

'Oh, Twiddle! That's the second time you've forgotten to pay that bill,' said Mrs Twiddle, banging the oven door.

'Well, I remembered EVERYTHING ELSE,' said Twiddle. 'Here are the bones for soup – and the sausages. . . .'

'Bones for soup? Are you mad, Twiddle?' said his little wife. 'I never said a word about bones for soup.'

'Oh well – perhaps you wanted bones for that dog next door you're so fond of,' said Twiddle huffily. 'How was I to know? And you *did* say sausages – it was down on. . . .'

Mrs Twiddle was now taking the things out of his basket in amazement. 'Bones – and pork sausages – and herrings. No wonder the cat was interested in your basket and came to make a fuss of you!'

She lifted out the chocolate cake and the crumpets. 'Goodness me! What in the world did you go and get these for? I *told* you I was baking cakes today! Twiddle, I really begin to think you've gone mad!'

She took out the toothpaste and the cotton wool.
'And look at these! You had a new tube of toothpaste yesterday – and, why all this cotton wool? Are
you going to stuff a cushion or something? And
TWIDDLE! Is that a coal hammer? Oh, Twiddle,
you'll be the death of me! You know we haven't any
coal – only a bit of coke and some wood!'

'Well,' began Twiddle, most annoyed, 'all these
things were down on your. . . .'

'Twiddle! You must have spent all the money I
gave you for the newspaper bill on these things!' said
Mrs Twiddle. 'It was my *housekeeping* money! It was
very wrong of you to do that. You can pay for them all
out of your own money!'

Twiddle was most alarmed. 'But I can't. I only
have enough to. . . .'

Mrs Twiddle burst into tears. 'Why did you get all
those things? Now I shall never, *never* be able to trust
you to go shopping again.'

There came a knock at the front door just then.
Twiddle went to see who it was, feeling very gloomy
indeed. A tall man stood there, dressed in a mackintosh. He beamed at Twiddle.

'I say,' he said, 'I'm very, very sorry – but I've
done something *so* silly.'

Twiddle was very, very glad to hear that someone
else could do silly things. He asked the man in at
once. 'It's like this,' said the man, standing in the
hall, 'I went to have a cup of coffee at the teashop –
and by mistake I took your mac when I went out. So

I've brought it back. It had your name in it. Did you by any chance take mine? They are very alike!'

Mrs Twiddle came out to hear what all the talking was about. She looked at the mac Twiddle had hung in the hall. 'Yes – he took yours!' she said. 'They *are* alike! Dear, dear – you men!'

'Good gracious!' said Twiddle, light dawning on him all at once. 'I smoked your pipe, then – and used your hanky – and oh, my word, I bought all the things on your shopping list!'

'No! Did you really?' said the tall man. 'You know, I tried to remember everything that was down, but I couldn't. I bought the chocolate cake and the crumpets – and I bought the bones for soup, and the sausages and the herrings. Was there anything else on the list?'

'Yes – toothpaste – cotton wool – and a coal hammer,' said Twiddle dolefully.

'My word!' said the man. 'I forgot all those. I *shall* get into trouble when I get back home. But do you *want* toothpaste and cotton wool and a coal hammer?'

'Of course not!' said Mrs Twiddle, answering for Twiddle. 'You can have them if you'd like to pay us for them.'

'Oh, I will, with pleasure,' said the man. 'It will save me going back to the shops. Dear, dear – I must have the worst memory in the world.'

'Yes – even worse than mine,' agreed Twiddle happily. 'Here's the hammer – toothpaste – and cotton wool.'

'I'm sorry you bought the other things,' said the man, paying out the money. 'But I've bought them, too, and I really couldn't face my wife with *two* chocolate cakes, *two* lots of sausages, *two*. . . .'

'No, no, of course not,' said Twiddle, who was not

at all anxious to hand over the cake, the crumpets and the rest.

The man took off Twiddle's mac, and Twiddle gave him the right one. They said goodbye, and out he went, his basket full.

Mrs Twiddle still looked very cross. Twiddle knew she had a lot more to say.

'Come into the sitting room, Twiddle,' said Mrs Twiddle, in a stern voice. 'I have something to say to you.' He followed her in, feeling very gloomy. She suddenly saw the three red roses in the vase.

'Wherever did those lovely flowers come from?' said Mrs Twiddle, and sniffed them in delight.

'I bought them for you,' said Twiddle, in a small voice.

'Red roses mean "I love you",' said Mrs Twiddle, her eyes shining.

'That's why I bought them,' said Twiddle. 'I may be a very silly husband, but I do think you are a nice little wife. So I bought you those roses.'

'Twiddle, you're a darling!' said Mrs Twiddle, and she gave him a very sudden hug. 'Now, when would you like the sausages? For supper? And I'll make some nice soup with those bones. And herrings will do fine for breakfast, because the kippers will keep. And we'll have a little tea party with those lovely crumpets and chocolate cake!'

Well, well, well! Twiddle simply couldn't understand the sudden change. But I can, can't you? After all, if somebody loves you very much, you can put up with quite a lot of silliness! Dear old Twiddle, I can't help liking him.

ENID BLYTON

If you are an eager Beaver reader, perhaps you ought to try some of our exciting Enid Blyton titles. They are available in bookshops or they can be ordered directly from us. Just complete the form below, enclose the right amount of money and the books will be sent to you at home.

☐	THE CHILDREN OF CHERRY-TREE FARM	£1.99
☐	THE CHILDREN OF WILLOW FARM	£1.99
☐	NAUGHTY AMELIA JANE	£1.50
☐	AMELIA JANE AGAIN	£1.50
☐	THE BIRTHDAY KITTEN	£1.50
☐	THE VERY BIG SECRET	£1.50
☐	THE ADVENTUROUS FOUR	£1.50
☐	THE ADVENTUROUS FOUR AGAIN	£1.50
☐	THE NAUGHTIEST GIRL IS A MONITOR	£1.95
☐	THE NAUGHTIEST GIRL IN THE SCHOOL	£1.95
☐	THE ENCHANTED WOOD	£1.99
☐	THE WISHING-CHAIR AGAIN	£1.99
☐	HURRAH FOR THE CIRCUS	£1.75

If you would like to order books, please send this form, and the money due to:
ARROW BOOKS, BOOKSERVICE BY POST, PO BOX 29, DOUGLAS, ISLE OF MAN, BRITISH ISLES. Please enclose a cheque or postal order made out to Arrow Books Ltd for the amount due including 22p per book for postage and packing both for orders within the UK and for overseas orders.

NAME ....

ADDRESS ....

....

Please print clearly.

Whilst every effort is made to keep prices low it is sometimes necessary to increase cover prices at short notice. Arrow Books reserve the right to show new retail prices on covers which may differ from those previously advertised in the text or elsewhere.

BEAVER BESTSELLERS

You'll find books for everyone to enjoy from Beaver's bestselling range—there are hilarious joke books, gripping reads, wonderful stories, exciting poems and fun activity books. They are available in bookshops or they can be ordered directly from us. Just complete the form below and send the right amount of money and the books will be sent to you at home.

☐ THE ADVENTURES OF KING ROLLO	David McKee	£2.50
☐ MR PINK-WHISTLE STORIES	Enid Blyton	£1.95
☐ FOLK OF THE FARAWAY TREE	Enid Blyton	£1.99
☐ REDWALL	Brian Jacques	£2.95
☐ STRANGERS IN THE HOUSE	Joan Lingard	£1.95
☐ THE RAM OF SWEETRIVER	Colin Dann	£2.50
☐ BAD BOYES	Jim and Duncan Eldridge	£1.95
☐ ANIMAL VERSE	Raymond Wilson	£1.99
☐ A JUMBLE OF JUNGLY JOKES	John Hegarty	£1.50
☐ THE RETURN OF THE ELEPHANT JOKE BOOK	Katie Wales	£1.50
☐ THE REVENGE OF THE BRAIN SHARPENERS	Philip Curtis	£1.50
☐ THE RUNAWAYS	Ruth Thomas	£1.99
☐ EAST OF MIDNIGHT	Tanith Lee	£1.99
☐ THE BARLEY SUGAR GHOST	Hazel Townson	£1.50
☐ CRAZY COOKING	Juliet Bawden	£2.25

If you would like to order books, please send this form, and the money due to:

ARROW BOOKS, BOOKSERVICE BY POST, PO BOX 29, DOUGLAS, ISLE OF MAN, BRITISH ISLES. Please enclose a cheque or postal order made out to Arrow Books Ltd for the amount due including 22p per book for postage and packing both for orders within the UK and for overseas orders.

NAME ....

ADDRESS ....

....

Please print clearly.

Whilst every effort is made to keep prices low it is sometimes necessary to increase cover prices at short notice. Arrow Books reserve the right to show new retail prices on covers which may differ from those previously advertised in the text or elsewhere.

BEAVER BOOKS FOR YOUNGER READERS

Have you heard about all the exciting stories available in Beaver? You can buy them in bookstores or they can be ordered directly from us. Just complete the form below and send the right amount of money and the books will be sent to you at home.

☐	THE BIRTHDAY KITTEN	Enid Blyton	£1.50
☐	THE WISHING CHAIR AGAIN	Enid Blyton	£1.99
☐	BEWITCHED BY THE BRAIN SHARPENERS	Philip Curtis	£1.75
☐	SOMETHING NEW FOR A BEAR TO DO	Shirley Isherwood	£1.95
☐	REBECCA'S WORLD	Terry Nation	£1.99
☐	CONRAD	Christine Nostlinger	£1.50
☐	FENELLA FANG	Ritchie Perry	£1.95
☐	MRS PEPPERPOT'S OUTING	Alf Prøysen	£1.99
☐	THE WORST KIDS IN THE WORLD	Barbara Robinson	£1.75
☐	THE MIDNIGHT KITTENS	Dodie Smith	£1.75
☐	ONE GREEN BOTTLE	Hazel Townson	£1.50
☐	THE VANISHING GRAN	Hazel Townson	£1.50
☐	THE GINGERBREAD MAN	Elizabeth Walker	£1.50
☐	BOGWOPPIT	Ursula Moray Williams	£1.95

If you would like to order books, please send this form, and the money due to:

ARROW BOOKS, BOOKSERVICE BY POST, PO BOX 29, DOUGLAS, ISLE OF MAN, BRITISH ISLES. Please enclose a cheque or postal order made out to Arrow Books Ltd for the amount due including 22p per book for postage and packing both for orders within the UK and for overseas orders.

NAME ....

ADDRESS ....

....

Please print clearly.

Whilst every effort is made to keep prices low it is sometimes necessary to increase cover prices at short notice. Arrow Books reserve the right to show new retail prices on covers which may differ from those previously advertised in the text or elsewhere.